"YOU WILL DIE, WHITE EYES," MEDICINE BEAR SNAPPED, HIS FACE TWISTING UP IN RAGE.

—————————— ✳ ——————————

"We'll all die someday," Calhoun replied.

"During our journey, you will die," Medicine Bear corrected himself.

Calhoun shrugged as he lit the cigarette. "I promised the major I'd get you to Fort Kearny," Calhoun said ominously. "I didn't promise him you'd be alive when I got you there."

Medicine Bear's eyes looked like small coals. He had been insulted like that by a white man once before. It took the white man two full days and one night to die. And he did not die bravely. Medicine Bear thought it would be interesting to apply the same things to this hard-eyed white man. Then he looked into Calhoun's eyes and the smallest chill ran up his back, for he saw the immense hatred he had for white men reflected in Calhoun's eyes.

ALSO BY CLINT HAWKINS

SADDLE TRAMP
THE CAPTIVE
GUNPOWDER TRAIL
GOLD AND LEAD
BANDIT'S BLOOD

Published by
HarperPaperbacks

SADDLE TRAMP

SIOUX TRAIL

———————— ✱ ————————

CLINT HAWKINS

HarperPaperbacks
A Division of HarperCollinsPublishers

HarperPaperbacks   *A Division of* HarperCollins*Publishers*
10 East 53rd Street, New York, N.Y. 10022

Copyright © 1993 by HarperCollins*Publishers*
All rights reserved. No part of this book may be used or reproduced in any manner whatsoever without written permission of the publisher, except in the case of brief quotations embodied in critical articles and reviews. For information address HarperCollins*Publishers,*
10 East 53rd Street, New York, N.Y. 10022.

Cover illustration by John Thompson

First printing: October 1993

Printed in the United States of America

•

HarperPaperbacks and colophon are trademarks of HarperCollins*Publishers*

❖ 10 9 8 7 6 5 4 3 2 1

CHAPTER

* 1 *

Wade Calhoun's bony old horse just sort of keeled over and died, with one last grand flurry of flatulence.

Calhoun, who had been standing alongside the animal trying to figure out what was afflicting it, barely managed to skip out of the way as the horse flopped over.

"Christ Almighty," Calhoun breathed, more in awe than in anger. The latter would come later, sure as the sun rose in the east. Wade Calhoun was not the most temperate of men at the best of times. Something like this was bound to set him off sooner or later. But for now, he was just amazed at the horse. It was almost humorous, but Calhoun was not laughing. Not when he was out here in the middle of nowhere.

He looked down at the horse and realized it wasn't really dead after all. It struggled and flapped, trying futilely to stand. Calhoun tried helping the horse up, tugging at the reins. He did it to more easily get his fancy Spanish saddle off the animal than by any wish to help it. His poor luck with horses was almost legendary across the west, and he knew that he could be of little real help to the animal now.

His efforts were as futile as the horse's, and he gave up just before the horse did. The beast's nostrils were flared and its eyes wide. It seemed to know it was dying.

"Damn," Calhoun muttered. Whatever humor he might have found in the situation had rapidly fled. He pulled one of his Colt Dragoons and calmly shot the horse in the head. Because of his poor luck with horses, Wade Calhoun never ever formed a master-pet relationship with one. Still, he could feel something for an animal that had done its best. Hence the bullet to put the dying animal out of its misery.

Calhoun slid the Dragoon into the cross-draw holster. He wore two of them that way, each housing a Dragoon. Then he sighed. "Damn, why does this shit always happen when there ain't a damn thing around?" he mused aloud. He was irked by the truthfulness of the statement, though. Such things never happened to him on the outskirts of a town. No, that would never happen. Instead, they always happened when he was miles from any place where he could get help.

The horse had been showing signs that something was afflicting it for several days. The splotchy bay had been rolling and pawing the ground regularly, indicating that it was suffering some stomach ailment. As the days passed Calhoun had tried to push the horse a little more, hoping he could make Fort Laramie. He had no idea of what to do for the creature; anything he had ever tried to do to help an animal had instead made its suffering worse.

Despite Calhoun's eagerness to push for the fort, the horse showed less and less energy. Finally, after it stumbled several times, Calhoun had dismounted, wondering what to do. He was still checking the animal out when it keeled over.

Calhoun looked around, figuring he was still two days' ride from Fort Laramie. Without a horse, he was looking at four days, maybe more.

The rage finally overcame him, and he kicked the dead horse. "Goddamn stupid hunk of buzzard goddamn bait," he snapped.

Then he sighed. Such displays of anger would get him nowhere. He had to get moving, though. He was in country crisscrossed by war parties of Sioux, Arikaras, Pawnees, Kaws, and more. While Calhoun hated and wanted to kill Indians, the Sioux most of all, he had no desire to meet any out here on the barren plains.

First, he had to get his saddle, no easy task with the deadweight of the horse lying on one side of it. Calhoun was about five-foot-ten and one hundred seventy pounds. Not a very large man, all in all, but his lanky, wiry frame belied the strength of his long, ropelike muscles.

With little enthusiasm, Calhoun bent and undid the cinch. He drew his big bowie knife and hacked off the horse's head. It took some doing, though the blade was big and well sharpened. When he was done, he wiped the knife blade clean on the horse's hide and slipped the knife back into the sheath, which dangled like a shoulder holster under his left arm, snug against his body. The tip of the sheath was tied to his belt to keep it from flopping around.

He pulled the Greener shotgun out of the saddle scabbard on top of the horse and removed the fulminate of mercury caps. Then, using the scatter-gun as a lever and the horse's severed head as the fulcrum, he managed to raise the horse's torso enough with one arm so that he could jerk the saddle back and forth, working it out from under the animal with his other hand.

Sweat broke out on his forehead and dripped down off his long, slim nose to splatter on the fine leather of the saddle. It was not easy work, but finally he was done.

Puffing hard and coated with sweat, Calhoun dropped the saddle and plopped his buttocks on the horse's body. He ran a sleeve across his forehead. With arms shaking a little from the effort to free the saddle, he pulled out his fixings and rolled a cigarette. He fired it up and smoked it down, letting his body return to normal.

Finally he flicked the cigarette into a pool of blood and watched without interest as it sputtered and hissed a second before dying. Everything seemed to be dying on him, he thought ironically, except himself. He knew that back in his mind somewhere he had been trying to die for a while—ever since Lizbeth and Lottie had been killed and butchered. Trouble was, he was too good at surviving, and he knew that even further down in his head somewhere, his instincts and abilities were keeping him alive. He wasn't sure how he felt about that, but since he couldn't change it anyway, he tried not to think of it.

He stood and stretched, looking to the west with irritation. He could see a storm heading his way, and it would not be long in arriving. He pulled his slicker out of his saddlebags and set it aside. Then he got his cleaning kit and patiently cleaned, oiled, and reloaded both the pistol and the shotgun. Then he put his supplies away.

He glanced at the westering sky again. He figured an hour, maybe two before the storm hit him. He pulled the slicker on with a shrug. Making sure his battered old slouch hat was set tightly on his head, he hauled the saddle up onto his left shoulder. Its weight was considerable, but he would as soon leave his boots behind as the saddle. It—along with his weapons—was his only real possession. It was hand-tooled leather inlaid with threads of silver. The saddle horn was almost as large as a small dinner plate. He had large, tooled-leather *tapaderos,* covering the stirrups. Each side had a saddle holster encasing a big Colt Walker, and a saddle scabbard, one containing the 10-gauge Greener shotgun and the other a Henry single-shot rifle. With the bedroll and full saddlebags, it was heavy.

Calhoun marched off, heading north, hoping he could make Chugwater Creek before the storm hit. He was still some miles away when the sky darkened almost to black. Less than five minutes later big, fat, heavy drops were falling. That swiftly changed to a noisy rainstorm, with sharp twigs of lightning flickering down from the heavens and great grumbling rolls of thunder shaking the earth.

Calhoun continued doggedly plodding along, half hoping that a bolt of lightning would strike him and end his misery once and for all. But it did not.

Despite the fact that it was still pouring, he felt a touch of relief when he reached the Chugwater.

Brush and trees—cottonwoods and willows mostly—lined the bubbling ribbon of water. The thick, tangled brush was hard to push through, but that and the canopy of leaves offered some protection from the bullying wind and the pounding rain.

Calhoun managed to get a small fire going, but it was barely enough to allow him a watered-down, tepid mug of coffee to wash down a few bone-dry, leathery strips of buffalo jerky. Then the rain found even the pitiful little fire and washed it into oblivion.

None of this improved Calhoun's sour mood. He rolled a cigarette and smoked it down, cupping the tiny flickering coal at the end. He flicked the smoldering butt out into the rain and spread his bedroll out under some brush. He crawled inside and burrowed as deeply as he could, trying to keep more rain off his head. The old slouch hat certainly hadn't kept him dry.

With a growl of annoyance at the world—and at himself—he slid into sleep.

Morning brought precious little relief from the storm. The rain had slackened some, but the day was still gray, leaden, and soggy. Thick mist swirled up from the creek and seemed to cling with filmy tentacles to the trees and brush.

"Goddamn rain," Calhoun mumbled, "Goddamn horses. Goddamn every goddamn thing."

Calhoun was certain he would find no better shelter from the storm than he had here, so he figured he would make himself a little more comfortable and wait the poor weather out. He pushed through the thicket and the chill mist. He finally found a small dead cottonwood. Animals had hollowed out the bottom of the trunk, leaving behind some punk-like material. Calhoun figured it would do.

He went back and retrieved his gear. Then he prowled around, looking under thick brush for wood, while remaining on the lookout for rattlesnakes.

He established a small pile of firewood and then started a fire in the hollowed-out tree. The punk left there had made the starting fairly easy. That done, he filled his small coffeepot with water and some Arbuckle's coffee beans he had pounded into submission. He set the pot near the fire and pulled out his last bit of bacon and the small sack of beans. He placed them in his little frying pan and left that to cook.

The small, but warm and filling meal, plus two cups of hot, harsh coffee cheered him a little. He knew he'd be in trouble soon, though, if the rain didn't let up. He was down to a few strips of jerky and some cornmeal, and that wouldn't last long.

"Hell with it," he said with a shrug. He would worry about food when he got hungry. Which wouldn't be long, considering how far he had walked yesterday and the fact that he didn't have a whole lot to do except sit and think about food.

It rained off and on throughout the day. Relief of a sort came in the late afternoon. Bits of sun began to dot the countryside, and Calhoun figured he would be able to pull out in the morning. He pored through his saddlebags and came up with an old piece of twine and a fishhook. He put a touch of cornmeal in the frying pan and mixed it with a few drops of water. Then he rolled the cornmeal into small balls and attached one to his fishhook, which was tied onto the twine, which in turn was tied to a stick. He tossed his makeshift fishing pole into the creek and leaned back against the soggy bark of a willow.

He felt lucky to pull in two good-sized catfish and called it quits for the day. He gutted the fish and cooked them and some crudely made biscuits. He ate with little enjoyment, though. He had never cared for fish, especially catfish. To him they always tasted of mud and decay. But it was a lot better than eating nothing. After eating, he smoked a cigarette and then stretched out in his bedroll.

Not a cloud disturbed the morning's blue sky. With a little more enthusiasm than he had shown the night before, Calhoun ate the last of the catfish and poor bread. He packed his things hurriedly, suddenly wanting to be on the move. Just before leaving, he checked his weapons. Then he hauled his saddle up and marched off.

He got only a little wet when he made his way across the creek, via several almost flat rocks. Then he was striding northward, sort of following the twisting Chugwater Creek. Sand hills or thick brush drove him away from the water from time to time. He also moved across country at times to avoid the creek's tighter twists.

He was getting mighty hungry along about midday when he heard the distinctive snuffling grunt of buffalo off to the west. With slightly renewed zest, he headed in that direction.

Minutes later he was cautiously making his way up a short grassy ridge. He stopped at the crest, looking over the small herd of buffalo. He nodded when he felt the breath of a breeze on his face. The buffalo would not smell him as he made his way toward the herd. Getting closer to the animals was necessary, since he was better than three hundred yards away. He was a good rifle shot, but he did not delude himself into thinking he could drop one of the big shaggies from way up here.

When he was within a hundred yards of the bison, they began getting a little edgy. Buffalo couldn't see worth a damn, Calhoun knew from experience. But their hearing and sense of smell were extremely good. He stopped and eased his saddle down onto the grass. He pulled the tail of his shirt out of his pants and wiped his face with it. The day was hot, though the humidity was down after the storm had moved on. Still, it was hotter than the devil's cookfire.

He wiped his hands on his pants and pulled out the Henry rifle. He checked it quickly, then knelt and aimed. A moment later, in the wake of the thunderous crack of the rifle, a fair-sized buffalo cow lay kicking in the dust.

Calhoun reloaded his rifle and put it away. With a weary sigh, he hefted his saddle yet again and headed toward his prey. Near the buffalo, he suddenly yelled and flapped his hat. The bison didn't wait to see what was causing all the ruckus; they just rumbled off, looking for some peaceful pasturage.

"Dumb bastards," Calhoun said as he arrived at his soon-to-be meal.

CHAPTER

* 2 *

Calhoun dropped his saddle next to the twitching carcass. He debated for a few moments whether he should stay here for a while or just carve out some meat and press on. His stomach won the debate, so he quickly looked around for dried buffalo dung. It was a little difficult to find because of all the rain in the past couple of days. Still, the day of hot sunshine had done its work well enough for Calhoun to find sufficient fuel for a small fire.

Back at his buffalo, he dropped the dung. He had used such buffalo chips many a time. It burned hot, but it also burned fast, and Calhoun wanted to make sure he had enough meat butchered out for his meal before starting the fire.

He set about his bloody work, deft hands working swiftly. Suddenly an arrow landed in the carcass not far from his hand. Calhoun instantly vaulted over the carcass and slid his legs out full and half rolled so he was on his stomach, looking over the buffalo. He had a pistol in his hand, having drawn it without thinking.

Two Indians popped up from a small coulee and began walking cautiously toward him. Each had a bow in his left hand. The bows were nocked, but not drawn back. All it would take to rectify that, though, was bringing the bow and arrow up with the left hand and drawing back the string with the right.

Calhoun waited, sweat curling down his pocked face. He wanted to drop these two Sioux straight off. He refrained, though. There might be other warriors around, and until he was sure, he could not risk killing these two. Besides, they would have horses. He might be able to buy one from them, if they were of a mind. Or he could kill them when he knew where their horses were and then go take the animals.

Neither of the young Sioux looked particularly threatening at the moment. With a mental shrug, Calhoun stood, holding the cocked Dragoon down alongside his right left. "You boys want somethin'?" he asked as the two warriors closed the distance.

The Sioux said nothing, which irked Calhoun all the more. The two stopped a few feet from him. Neither was more than sixteen, Calhoun figured. One wore a plain, long buckskin shirt, buckskin breechcloth, and buckskin leggings. The other wore buckskin leggings, and a breechcloth made of blanket. His torso was bare.

"Why you take my buffalo?" War Shirt, as Calhoun thought of him, said. His accent was thick, but his command of English was far better than Calhoun's abilities in Sioux.

"Ain't yours," Calhoun said. He was always sparing of speech, and didn't see that at the moment more was needed.

"My arrow," the young man said, pointing.

Calhoun waved his pistol in the general direction of the buffalo behind him. "My bullet," he said.

"This buffalo mine," War Shirt said arrogantly.

Calhoun was unafraid. Both warriors were too close to him now to be able to use their bows effectively. And he still had his cocked pistol in hand. If they tried to jump him, both would learn to regret it in a real hurry. "Bullshit," Calhoun said evenly.

The warrior started, and his eyes narrowed in anger.

"You boys got horses?" Calhoun asked.

The question seemed to surprise and confuse the two Indians. "Yes," Bare Chest said.

"I'll tell you what," Calhoun said easily. "You boys give me one of your ponies, and I'll give you the whole goddamn buffalo—'cept for a few pounds of meat."

The warriors looked at him blankly, as if they did not understand a word he had said. Calhoun knew better, though. He shrugged. "Ain't no skin off my ass," he said calmly. "But if you boys ain't interested in a swap, you best get gone."

The two Sioux looked at each other and exchanged a few words that Calhoun could not understand. Then War Shirt shrugged. "We got no ponies to trade," he said.

"Then git," Calhoun ordered.

The same Sioux nodded. "My arrow."

"You can get it."

War Shirt moved up and bent over. He grabbed the shaft of the arrow with his left and pulled. At the same time he half spun toward Calhoun, who was only a foot away. He tore out his knife and in the same motion tried to ram it into Calhoun's guts.

Calhoun had suspected the Sioux would try

something, so he was not taken completely unawares. But they were two against his one, and he could not count these warriors lightly. Not when both had scalps dangling from their bows.

Calhoun stepped toward War Shirt, surprising the warrior, and War Shirt's knife swept around Calhoun, just nicking his side. Calhoun managed to get his Dragoon up and fire it. War Shirt grunted softly. Calhoun knew he had wounded the man, but didn't know how badly.

War Shirt pulled back his knife for another try at stabbing Calhoun.

Calhoun was acutely aware of Bare Chest, who had dropped his bow as useless in such close-in fighting, moving toward him. He jerked his knee up, giving War Shirt a glancing blow in the groin. The Sioux hissed and went limp for a moment. Calhoun shoved as hard as he could, pushing War Shirt away.

Then Bare Chest slammed into Calhoun. They both tumbled over the buffalo carcass. "Damn," Calhoun hissed as the impact knocked his Dragoon out of his grasp.

Neither man could keep a grip on the other, and so both scrambled to get up before the other. Bare Chest was a little quicker and aimed a foot at Calhoun's head.

Calhoun dodged the main part of the kick, and Bare Chest's moccasin grazed his left temple. In getting out of the way, though, Calhoun had fallen again. He landed on the buffalo, almost puncturing himself on one of the horns.

Bare Shirt was closing in on him, his knife in hand. A cruel grin splitting the warrior's flat, bronze face.

"Son of a bitch," Calhoun said to himself. He clawed for the Dragoon, seeming to be moving as if he were caught in a lake of molasses. Bare Chest was barely a foot away, and was bending toward him when Calhoun finally got the pistol out, cocking it at the same time.

Calhoun fired. Bare Chest's eyes widened in surprise as a chunk of his spine was blown out his back from the impact of the .44-caliber slug at such close range. He fell atop Calhoun.

With a shout of rage, War Shirt leaped over the buffalo, landing on his friend and Calhoun. But in doing so, he could not bring his blade into play. He pushed himself up and grabbed Bare Chest's hair, trying to tug his friend out of the way.

He tripped over the buffalo's hump and lost his grip on Bare Chest. He struggled frantically to get back to his feet.

Calhoun used the opportunity to get up. "Don't," he warned.

The Sioux looked at the muzzle of that .44. Then he opened his mouth and began his death chant. He picked his knife up and stood, eyes never leaving Calhoun's. His chanting grew in volume and urgency. He flung himself wildly at this hard-looking white man.

Calhoun fired twice within a heartbeat. The balls punched War Shirt back a little, and then he crumpled to the ground. His chanting faded, and then disappeared.

Calhoun warily checked both Indians. They were dead. He retrieved his other Dragoon. Then he turned very slowly in a circle. There seemed to be no other Indians about. He began to relax a little. He still watched the land around him as he reloaded both Colts.

Once that was done, he pondered his options. He could go look for the Sioux ponies now, but he was virtually certain that predators would move in on his buffalo. He could sit here and eat, then go look for the horses, but the Indian ponies might wander off, especially since scavengers would be attracted by these three rotting carcasses—one animal and two human. The third possibility was to finish butchering the meat and then pack some of it along while he looked for the horses. That was the least appealing idea, since he had spent some time gathering fuel and his stomach was gnawing at him with hungry intensity.

With a sigh, he made his choice. He might not like it, but it made the most sense. Calhoun grabbed his knife.

The work went swiftly, albeit bloodily, and soon he was moving at a good pace north and a little east. The creek was down that way, and he thought there was a good chance that the two Sioux had left their ponies there to make sure they had water and graze.

After an hour of fruitless searching for the horses, he stopped near the creek. A heavy thatch of thorny brush almost blocked his progress completely, but Calhoun found a thin animal trail leading to the creek. Where he was, back from the creek a few feet, cottonwoods and willows grew heavily. He dropped his saddle, irked again that he would once more have to gather fuel for a fire. At least, he told himself, there was meat to eat, and a fair portion of it, too.

He set the saddle down and stood there a few moments rolling his shoulders and stretching, trying to loosen at least some of the tightness in his chest, shoulders, and back. Then he went looking for wood.

The search went smoothly, and soon he was squatting beside a good wood fire with buffalo meat sizzling in his pan and coffee bubbling in his little pot.

He ate with more gusto than he had shown in a while, digging hungrily into the fried buffalo tongue and some hump meat. Along with coffee, the meal was as good as any he had ever eaten while on his own. He was not much of a cook, and hated doing it. But he led such a solitary life that he did it most of the time.

After eating, he leisurely smoked a cigarette and sipped coffee. He was as content as he could be under the circumstances. He did wonder about the Indian horses, though. They should've been nearby, he figured. He finally concluded that the two warriors did not have any horses. He half suspected that they had come out here on foot on a horse-raiding expedition, maybe against the Pawnees or one of the other less nomadic tribes in the central plains. He finally rolled into his blankets and shut out his rising temper and irritation.

Calhoun kept a good lookout for the Indian

ponies—and for more Indians. He saw neither, being disappointed at not seeing horses, but relieved that he encountered no more Indians.

The meat he had taken lasted only through that day. For one thing, he couldn't carry all that much as well as the saddle and all. Another problem was that the meat went rancid quickly in this blazing heat.

The heat, too, made the walking difficult, even for a man with Calhoun's iron constitution and will. He was bathed in sweat after he had gone barely a quarter mile. The heat sapped him of his strength, and he called it a day earlier than he usually would.

The day after was even worse as far as traveling went. Still, he brought down one of the speedy pronghorn antelopes. He had found the goatlike-tasting meat to be pleasant, as long as he did not eat it too often.

In addition, he figured he was getting fairly close to Fort Laramie by now. He estimated that in one good day of walking—maybe two or even three at that slower pace he was keeping—he could reach it.

He made only five or six miles the next day, as the blistering blot of a sun pummeled the prairie and burned right through the top of Calhoun's slouch hat to fry his brain. In disgust with his "weakness," he quit early and found a reasonably comfortable spot. Then, telling himself that he would stay a few days and gather his strength, he made his camp.

Calhoun stayed there three days, hunting a little, resting, and keeping to the shade of the scraggly, heat-battered trees.

On the fourth day, with somewhat renewed spirits, he marched confidently out of his little camp and across the sere, wind- and sun-blasted prairie. He went northwest, leaving the creek behind as he made his way toward the Laramie River. The creek and the river came together somewhere up ahead, he knew, just as the Laramie flowed into the North Platte a little farther on. He figured the Laramie might have more traffic near it, what with wagon trains, soldiers, and Indians all making their way across this vast area.

He saw no one, though, and thought ironically that everyone else had enough sense to stay out of such blistering sun and heat. But no, not him; he marched blithely on as the heat shimmered up from the brown, dying grass. More than once he was plagued by mirages, until he learned to ignore them.

Calhoun made the Laramie River late in the day and gratefully found a place that was somewhat comfortable and seemed to have not been used much. He had shot another antelope that day, and he feasted well on its gamy flesh. He was out of coffee, though.

As he slid into his bedroll that night he told himself firmly that he would make Fort Laramie tomorrow, or else. He didn't know what "or else" referred to, only that he had to say it.

CHAPTER
✱ 3 ✱

Wade Calhoun struggled up another of the interminable grassy ridges, but he showed a little more enthusiasm, if not speed, on this one, since he was certain that Fort Laramie was right beyond it. Not that this ridge looked any different from the others he had already crossed. He knew because he had been hearing fort noises—the blacksmith's hammer being one of the most prominent—for some time.

He reached the top of the grassy, gently rounded ridge and stopped, looking over the scene before him. As he had known, the fort was spread out to the west—his left—a little. Around the fort were tipis, mostly Sioux, Calhoun figured. These were the same proud, haughty Sioux warriors who controlled everything from the Platte River hills to the Missouri River and from the foothills of the Rockies to Minnesota Territory. The finely painted tipis spoke eloquently of their power and influence.

Calhoun figured the Indians were there to get the annual payment of goods and supplies that had been promised them in the Fort Laramie treaty a few years ago. That was the only thing Calhoun could think of that would have the Sioux living even temporarily in the shadow of the fort. Calhoun wished that the fort's cannon would open fire on the sprawling village. The Sioux should be made to suffer as much as possible.

As he stood there looking down the ridge, visions of a Kansas Territory farmstead danced in his mind. Pictures of the smoldering ruins of a house, of blood, of bodies lying in broken emptiness.

"Shit," Calhoun muttered, drawing in a ragged breath. He set his saddle down and pulled out his fixings. It was always that way for him. Almost anything he saw reminded him in some way or another of his family—his beautiful Lizbeth and his darling infant Lottie—butchered by rampaging Sioux warriors. Though years had passed, the pain was still as fresh as it was the day he had found them. Since that day, he had carried around in him a hatred that was as much a part of him as his heart and lungs, his arms and legs.

He fought the urge to walk down the ridge, the two big Colt Walkers in hand, and the Dragoons still ready in their holster, and start blasting any and all Indians he saw. He felt nothing but loathing for them. He even hated the crying children, maybe them most of all, after what these people had done to him.

He dropped the cigarette butt and squashed it under the toe of his boot. He could feel the burning tip for a moment, so worn were his boot soles. "God-damn Sioux anyhow," Calhoun muttered under his breath.

He hoisted the saddle again and began moving slowly down the slope. As he neared the first of the tipis, though, he straightened his back and squared his shoulders. There was no way in heaven or hell that he would let these Indians see him slumping.

By the time he tramped through the gates of Fort Laramie, he was in a foul humor. It wasn't bad enough he had been on his feet since the day before the birth of time. No, he had to spend an hour or so moving through the scattered Sioux camp. That really kept his blood boiling.

Calhoun ignored the soldiers and Indians staring at him, though he was conscious of their scrutiny. He felt a bit of relief inside that it was so late in the season now that all the wagon trains had long since passed by.

He walked up the three stairs to the building in which the fort commander had his office. A tall, red-faced private stood at parade rest in front of the door. He snapped to attention as Calhoun made his way up the stairs.

"Can I help you?" the soldier asked, his brogue giving away his Irish ancestry.

"I'd like to see Major Mangum," Calhoun said wearily.

"The major is busy, sir," the soldier said pompously.

"Fine," Calhoun said as if he had not heard the private. "Just go and tell him Wade Calhoun'd like to see him."

"The major told me he was not to be disturbed by anyone."

Calhoun nodded. Then he suddenly grabbed a fistful of the private's wool blouse. He jerked backward, pulling the surprised soldier. In one flowing move, he spun and shoved the soldier away.

One of the soldier's heels went off the top step, and he fell, landing in the dust. He yelped twice: once when he began to fall, and again when he landed. His rifle clacked to the ground a couple feet away. The private scrambled for it.

"Uh-uh," Calhoun warned. He had kept moving when the soldier fell, drawing one of his Dragoons, cocking it. Now he stood facing the soldier, Dragoon centered on the man's chest. He still held his saddle and gear over his other shoulder.

The private froze, fear splashing over him like water over a falls.

The door behind Calhoun burst open. "What the hell is going on here?" Mangum began. He stopped and grinned. "Wade," he said, voice suddenly friendly.

"Major," Calhoun said evenly, not looking behind him.

Mangum took in the tableau before him. "You fixing to kill Private O'Shea?" he asked. He sounded almost as if such a thing did not matter.

"If I have to."

Private Ian O'Shea still sat in the dirt, arms behind him, holding his back up from the ground a little. His face was coated with sweat, eyes worried.

"What started this, Private?" Mangum demanded.

O'Shea lifted a hand and pointed to Calhoun. "He demanded to see you, sir. I told him you ordered me not to allow anyone in. Next thing I know, he grabs me and throws me down here." New fears joined the older ones. O'Shea figured he was damned no matter what happened. If he had let Calhoun in, and Calhoun was not as friendly with the major as he had hinted, O'Shea would have been in trouble. On the other hand, he had tried to follow his orders to the letter, and all that got him was a pain in the rear and a heaping dose of humiliation. He was certain he could not win in this situation.

Major Miles Mangum had been an army officer for much of his adult life. He loved the army, though he certainly could see things about it that he could fix. He had started as an enlisted man, but his meritorious service during the Mexican War had brought him to the officers' corps. As such, he knew army life from both perspectives. Now, as he looked down at O'Shea, he knew exactly what O'Shea was thinking, and he could not fault the private for his actions, though something might have to be said later about his readiness for battle. On the other hand, Wade Calhoun was one tough customer, which went a long way to mitigating the circumstances.

"Put the gun away, Wade," Mangum said. As Calhoun did so Mangum said, "Get up, Private, and go clean yourself up." He paused, waiting for O'Shea to rise. "You did right in following your orders, Private," the major said. One of the reasons he was well liked by his men was that he understood their problems and was no more dictatorial than he had to be. The troops admired that. He half smiled. "But next time be more prepared for trouble. Not everyone will give you notice of attack. Dismissed."

"Yes, sir," O'Shea said, relieved. He grabbed his rifle and hurried off.

"Sergeant Whitcomb," Mangum said, turning a little to the short, grizzled, barrel-chested noncom just to his right, "find someone to relieve Private O'Shea at guard duty. And, Sergeant," he continued after Whitcomb turned, "put the weapon away."

Sergeant Gerard Whitcomb, who had turned back to face Mangum again, nodded. "Yes, sir." He slid his Colt Dragoon to his flap holster. "Anything else, sir?"

"No, Sergeant." Mangum looked at Calhoun and grinned a little. Not only was he an efficient officer, he also had a sense of humor, something lacking far too often in military men. "Come on in, you old fart," he said.

Calhoun almost smiled, but that was not his way. He settled for a nod and walked into the office with Mangum right behind him. Just inside the door, Calhoun set his saddle down, grateful for having the burden gone.

Mangum took his seat behind the desk. Calhoun grabbed a chair and set it in front of the desk. He straddled it, leaning his forearms on the back, facing Mangum.

The major reached into a desk drawer and pulled out a tall, slim bottle and two tin mugs. He filled the mugs and corked the bottle, though he left it on the desk. Calhoun nodded and took a long swig. Mangum did the same. He pulled two cigars out of another drawer. He tossed one to Calhoun and lit the other for himself. Then he leaned back, placing his boots on the desk. He rested his mug lightly on his lower abdomen and waited until Calhoun had his cigar going.

"So, Wade, what the hell brings you to this god-forsaken hole?"

"Lookin' for work," Calhoun said without shame.

"You busted again?" Mangum asked with a smile.

"Yep." Had the question been asked by most men, Calhoun would've been offended and quite likely would have shot the individual. From Miles Mangum, though, he could not take exception at it.

"I suppose you're on foot, too?" Mangum questioned, chuckling a little.

Calhoun took a puff of the cigar and then studied the glowing tip of it for a minute. "Yep," he answered again.

Mangum laughed. "What happened this time?"

"Son of a bitch just up and died on me," Calhoun said dryly.

"What from?" Mangum asked, still laughing.

"Hell if I know," Calhoun said, coming as close to humor as he ever did. "All that damn nag did was fart. Slowed down considerably, too, near the end." He took a drink, not wanting to discuss the beast any further.

"He eat much?"

Calhoun shook his head.

"Pawed the ground or tried to roll on his back?"

Calhoun nodded. "A lot near the end." He wondered what Mangum was getting at.

"Your horse had some kind of colic," Mangum pronounced.

Calhoun shrugged. It didn't make any difference to him. The horse was dead and that was that. All the knowledge of what had killed it wouldn't bring it back to life. He puffed quietly on his cigar a bit and took a couple of drinks of whiskey. Then he asked, "So, you got any work for me?"

Mangum hesitated before answering. He had been thinking of how he might help Calhoun, who had once worked for him as a scout. But that was before Calhoun's family had been killed. The death of his family had turned him into a tough, humorless, and often vicious man. The major knew full well Calhoun's hatred of Indians, particularly the Sioux, and the job he was considering offering would put the former scout in close proximity to those Indians.

"I don't need no handouts, Major," Calhoun said. "You got no work for me, I'll head on elsewhere."

"Oh, I got a job for you, Wade. I just ain't certain you'll want it."

"I ain't been known for turnin' much down when it comes to work," Calhoun said levelly.

Mangum nodded. "I need some people escorted down to New Fort Kearny, and I can afford to send only two of my men."

"Why only two?"

"Jesus, half the damn garrison is down with dysentery or other ailments."

"Why do you need me? Seems to me two of your men could do it."

"Don't know as if I could trust them as much as I could you," Mangum said honestly. "Hell, Wade, you know these kind of boys well's I do. Immigrants and slum dwellers for the most part, come to the army to make something of themselves. They'll hightail it first chance they get, like as not."

Calhoun knew that for a fact, had seen it plenty back when he worked for the army regularly. He nodded. "So, what is it?"

Mangum sighed and pulled his boots off the desk. Then he leaned forward, set his mug down, and leaned his forearms on the desk. "Taking a Sioux leader to Fort Kearny to meet—"

"No," Calhoun snapped with finality. "No goddamn way."

"Hear me out, Wade. . . ."

"There's nothin' to hear, Major. You know how I feel about those bastards."

"Yes, I do," Mangum said. "But—"

"No buts," Calhoun said, temper boiling over. He wanted to rail at Mangum, ask the major what he was thinking of when he offered such a thing to him. While it was true he needed money, he didn't need it badly enough to take on such a loathsome task.

Calhoun drained his mug and set it on the desk. Then he pushed himself to his feet. "I'm obliged for the whiskey, and this," he said, holding out the cigar. "You mind if I spend the night here?" he asked, hating to do so. "I'll be gone at first light."

"Where to?"

Calhoun shrugged. He turned and stuck the cigar in his mouth. Grabbing his saddle, he strode outside. He headed left along the parade ground, watching with disinterest as troops drilled under the grueling hot sun.

He stopped outside the sutler's store and set his saddle down. Then he checked his supply of cash. He had less than thirty-eight dollars. It wasn't near enough to buy a horse, but he could get some new duds and some basic supplies. He could not get much in the way of food supplies anyway, seeing as how he would be on foot again. The thought did not cheer him any.

With an annoyed sigh, he grabbed his saddle and entered the store, appreciating its relative coolness and dimness after the heat and bright sun of the outside. He put the saddle down again, just to the left of the door.

"Wade. Wade Calhoun," the sutler said with a note of surprise. "How you been?"

"Just fine, Les. You?"

Lester Wallace shrugged and smiled. " 'Bout as good as ever." Wallace was a short, very round man, with a halo of close-cropped white hair around his otherwise bald head. He had been the sutler here for as long as Calhoun, who had done a fair amount of trade in this store, could remember. "Now," Wallace asked, "what can I do for you?"

CHAPTER

✱ 4 ✱

Calhoun picked out a pair of sturdy black denim pants, a simple collarless cotton shirt, a pair of heavy-duty calf-high boots, two pairs of plain socks, a union suit, three bandannas, and a pair of red suspenders.

"Best give him some soap, too, Les," someone behind Calhoun said with a lisp. His tone was not friendly.

"Keep your nose out of this, Sculley," Wallace advised.

"Go to hell, Les," Corporal Norm Sculley said, almost lightheartedly. "This son of a bitch stinks like fresh bear shit."

Wallace looked at Calhoun, fear and curiosity in his eyes. He knew the kind of man Calhoun was. He was not a friend—Wallace didn't think the former scout had any friends—but the sutler had dealt with him enough to know he was not the kind of man one wanted to mess with. Unless, of course, one was crazy. Wallace figured Sculley might qualify.

"Anything else, Mr. Calhoun?" the sutler asked.

"I'd like—"

Sculley shoved up alongside Calhoun at the low wood counter. He slapped some coins down on it.

"Hell, I'll even pay for the soap," he said, glaring over at Calhoun. "If'n it'll help clear the air 'round here."

Wallace blanched and stepped back from the counter. There was going to be bloodshed in a moment, sure as anything.

Calhoun looked at Sculley. The corporal was a big man, considerably larger in bulk, if not in height, than he. But much of his weight was flab. He had a harelip, which accounted for the lisp. He had several days' worth of growth on his face, which meant little, since Calhoun was in the same condition. A shaggy mustache, stained with tobacco, dropped over Sculley's top lip.

"Mighty generous of you, pal," Calhoun said evenly. "But I don't need your help."

Wallace heard the warning in his flat voice. Sculley did not.

Calhoun turned back to Wallace. "Now, as I was sayin', I—"

"Goddamn you," Sculley snapped, grabbing Calhoun's left sleeve, "you ain't gonna spit on my generosity."

Calhoun let himself be hauled partly around. "Then I'll spit on you, boy," he said. He blew a good-sized glob of spittle onto Sculley's face.

"Why you son of a bitch," Sculley snarled, wiping a sleeve across his face. "I'll—"

"You'll what, pus gut?" Calhoun asked.

Sculley's eyes were wide, and he gulped in worry. He tried not to breathe too much lest he get pricked by the sharp tip of Calhoun's bowie knife, which was lightly brushing his shirt an inch or so above his bellybutton.

"You suddenly forget how to flap that big hole in your face, lard ass?" Calhoun asked.

Sculley nodded nervously, licking his lips.

"Then get the hell out. And stay out. You poke your snout in here before I'm done, and I'll shoot it off."

The corporal nodded again, then sucked in a big breath, relieved that the bowie knife was no longer touching his abdomen. He waddled out.

Calhoun slid the knife away and turned to face Wallace, who was shaking his head at the stupidity of men. Especially bullies like Sculley.

"Now, Les, I'd like some soap." Had he been a man to smile even a little, Calhoun would have done so then. But he didn't. "And some sacking."

"For a towel?"

"Yep."

"I got some new. Real soft, too. Not like that scratchy old shit we got most of the time."

Calhoun nodded. "I reckon that'll be all for now."

"No powder or lead and such?" Wallace asked, surprised.

"I'll be by first thing tomorrow for such. Just before I pull out."

Wallace nodded and headed off to get the requested items. When he had everything on the counter, he toted the bill up and Calhoun paid him.

"You lookin' to take a scrub-up, Wade?" he asked as Calhoun reached for the small box containing his purchases.

"I'd thought on it."

"I got a room in my place I use for such at times. You're welcome to it."

"The river'll do." Calhoun did not like to be beholden to anyone.

"You'll be unprotected there." He nodded toward the door. "Sculley ain't the kind of man to forget such an insult as you gave him. He'll be lookin' for a payback."

Calhoun shrugged. "He don't scare me none."

"Never said he did. But with a bully like Sculley, you can expect him to come at you when you're not in much of a position to defend yourself any."

"Like takin' a bath in the river," Calhoun said with a nod.

"Precisely."

"Reckon I'll take you up on your offer, Mr. Wallace."

"Good." The sutler paused. "Where you plannin' to stay?"

Calhoun shrugged. "Just figured I'd stake out a chunk of ground over near the bakery."

"Hell, stay in my place. You'd not have to worry about your gear and such."

"It won't put you out none?"

"Not atall."

Calhoun didn't have to think about it. He could use a soft bed and the comfort of a roof over his head. "I'm obliged." He paused. "But I insist on payin' you."

"No," Wallace said flatly. "You've done good service for me back in the old days before . . . back in the old days. Your payment for this was paid back then."

Calhoun nodded.

He grabbed the box in his right hand and walked

toward the door. With a sigh of annoyance, he hoisted his saddle. There were times he wished he had never gotten the damn thing. This saddle had been more trouble than it was worth, more often than not. He sighed again. That was not true, and if a man had to have only one possession, he could do a lot worse than this saddle.

"Hold on there a minute, Wade," Wallace said. He came from behind the counter. "Let me carry that box for you." He took it and said, "Come on, follow me. We'll get you all set up."

"The store?"

"It'll keep." The two men stepped outside. Wallace turned and locked the door with a large key that dangled by twine from his belt.

Wallace's house was not big, but it had three rooms—four if you counted the help's quarters behind the kitchen. "Ruby," Wallace called as he entered. "Ruby!"

A tall, spare, gray-haired black woman came out of the kitchen wiping her hands on an apron. "Yassir, Massah Wallace?" Her eyes brightened just a little when she saw Calhoun. "Massah Calhoun," she said in surprise. She had always like Calhoun. He was one of the few men who had treated her and her kind with at least a minimum of respect. He had never talked down to her, never abused her like so many others had done. She had felt sorry for him, too, when great misfortune had struck his family. It had turned him into a hard, bitter man, though the few times she had seen him since, he still treated her kindly.

"Ruby," Calhoun said, touching the brim of his hat. "You're lookin' as pert and pretty as ever."

"Stop joshin' me, Massah Calhoun," she said with a shy smile. She had been a good-looking woman in her youth. She knew that. Many was the white man who had come for her specially, because of her beautiful face and her shapely figure. But that was so long ago. Now when she looked at her face in a mirror, all she could see were wrinkles, a worn face, and steely-gray hair.

"Stop gabbin', Ruby," Wallace said, not harshly. "Mr. Calhoun's gonna stay the night, so make up the bed in the spare room. But first, fill him the tub back there so's he can clean up."

"Yassir." Ruby took the box from Wallace's hands, her fingers brushing his. With a sigh, she turned toward the room. Wallace left.

"This way, Massah Calhoun," Ruby said. But her thoughts were on Lester Wallace. He was not an unkind master. Indeed, of the several masters she had had, he was about the best. He had come to her, too, when he was a young man and she a young woman. After the third time he had visited her, he bought her from her master. She had been with him ever since, and their relationship was more than just master-slave, though both were wise enough to keep it a secret.

Calhoun dropped his saddle in a corner of the room. Ruby set the box on the small chest of drawers. She dragged the small, oddly shaped tub away from the wall where it had been stored. "I's'll be right back, Massah Calhoun."

"Thank you, Ruby." Calhoun stood there a

moment looking at the doorway. He thought, as he had a number of times in the past, that Ruby must have been a beautiful young woman. He wondered what it would've been like to have been with her. He wondered if Wallace had been with her. Then he almost grinned. There was no doubt whatsoever that Wallace had.

Calhoun sat on the bed and pulled off his worn boots and tossed them aside. He stood and removed the sheathed bowie knife, tossing it on the bed. He was just peeling off his gun belt when Ruby reentered, carrying two buckets of steaming water.

Right behind her was a young woman, this one the color of *café au lait*. She also carried two full pails. Calhoun was struck by the young woman's beauty. She was fairly tall and had a regal look about her. Her *café au lait* skin was smooth and flawless, her tightly kinked hair short. Her forehead was high and broad, sweeping down to a long, aquiline nose. Her eyes were deep and expressive. Her teeth, when she smiled shyly at Calhoun, were white. Calhoun could not take his eyes off her. It had been a time since he had had a woman, and of the ones he had had of late, none could hold a candle to this one.

Ruby watched Calhoun out of the corner of her eye and smiled. She could've brought her son, Joshua, to help, but she wanted to see what effect her daughter, Naomi, had on Calhoun. She had figured it would be just about what it was.

The women left and returned three more times, each time dumping water into the tub. By then, Calhoun was down to his red long johns. As the women left again he stripped even those off and stepped into the tub. It was a small tub, and he was much too long for it. He leaned back against the one tall end and dangled his feet over the sides. He relaxed, glad he had taken Wallace up on his offer.

His hand snaked out for his gun belt, lying next to the tub, when he heard the doorknob rattle. He left the gun where it was when he saw the young black woman enter shyly. He was a little embarrassed at being naked in the water like this, but not too much.

Naomi came to the side of the tub and knelt. "Mama said I was to come and he'p you, if'n you was of a mind." Her deep eyes searched his. She was embarrassed, not because she felt poorly about herself, but because she had had too much attention turned on her by the slovenly soldiers of the fort. She found herself hoping that this tough-looking man with the scars of many a battle on his chest would accept her.

"I'd be obliged," Calhoun said through a suddenly constricted throat. His body reacted to his desire for this woman. Still, he was just a bit unsure if that was to be part of the help. He figured it was, but until he was sure, he would tread lightly.

Naomi stood and shucked off her plain cotton shift. She wore nothing underneath, and like before, she was barefoot. Her body, as her face, was smooth and flawless, with small, pointed breasts and long, lean legs.

Now Calhoun was certain of why she was here, and he could let himself relax.

Naomi knelt again and took up some soap. She began lathering up his chest. Calhoun closed his eyes, enjoying the feel of her soapy hands on him.

When he was clean, he stood, unembarrassed, and stepped out of the tub. Naomi dried him off with the sacking material. Suddenly Calhoun pulled her to him and kissed her hard. She responded eagerly. He dipped and then swept her up in his arms. Moments later he was placing her softly on the bed.

"What's your name?" Calhoun asked later, after they were lying there comfortable in each other's arms. He had realized that he didn't even know her name.

"Naomi."

"Pretty."

"Thank you, massah."

His face clouded angrily, then relaxed. "I ain't your master," he said evenly. He wanted no part in any such a thing. Much of his family back in Kentucky owned slaves, and if he had stayed there, he probably would've done the same. But he had left home early on, at odds with his father and most of his brothers. It had been a decade or so since then, and he had seen too much of the world to be comfortable with the thought of owning another human.

Naomi smiled. "You want me to stay?" she asked.

"At least for a little."

After the second time Calhoun chased Naomi out after telling her to come back that night. He dressed in his new clothes and headed out. Dusk was hovering, and the western sky was shot through with reds and pinks and odd purples. The temperature had dropped some, and the constant breeze brought a pleasant feel with it.

CHAPTER

* 5 *

Calhoun stepped inside the enlisted men's saloon. The saloon was in the same building as Wallace's store, but the door was around the corner. The saloon and store were separated by a thick wall.

As it usually was, Calhoun remembered, the place was packed. The room was small, and with all the men in it, it was hot and it stank.

Calhoun shoved through the crowd toward the small, plain bar. He bought a bottle of whiskey. Leaving the glass on the bar, he took the bottle and fought his way to one corner, where it seemed there was a bit of breathing room. He figured he should go outside to get away from all these folks, but he knew that Major Mangum was not keen on men drinking outside the saloon. That prohibition included civilians.

He leaned back against the wall and sipped from the bottle held in his left hand. Occasionally he would set it down to roll and light a smoke. The crowd began to thin a little, for which Calhoun was grateful, though he remained in his corner.

About an hour after Calhoun arrived, Sculley walked in with two other corporals. They were loud and piggish looking. Calhoun shook his head. He hated such swaggering bullies almost as much as he hated the Sioux. He kept his eyes on them, just in case. They seemed the type to cause trouble when they had superior numbers.

It didn't take long for Sculley to spot him. The two locked eyes for a moment before the corporal turned to his two companions. Then the other two glared at Calhoun. Finally the three proceeded toward Calhoun, shoving other men out of their way. Calhoun unhurriedly corked his whiskey bottle.

The three corporals stopped about six feet from him and spread out some. All looked pleased, figuring they had him boxed in.

"Glad to see you took my advice," Sculley said with a smirk.

"I don't take advice from peckerwoods."

Sculley's eyes narrowed. "I don't cotton to such insults," he said, the lisping twang revealing his Texan origins.

Calhoun shrugged.

Sculley was furious, especially since some soldiers were chuckling at him. All had stopped gabbing and were watching the scene play out.

"You ought to heed your own advice, boy," Calhoun said. "Damn, but you stink. Hell, I've smelt hog pens weren't as offensive as you." It was a long sentence from Calhoun, but he could not pass up the opportunity.

Furious, Sculley stepped up almost nose to nose with Calhoun. "One more insult and I'll mash your head," he said, expecting Calhoun to cower like most everyone else did when he leaned on them. He also figured he was close enough to the civilian to prevent him from pulling out either his knife or one of the Colt Dragoons at his waist.

"That so?" Calhoun asked sarcastically.

"That's so." Sculley sneered.

"Hmm," Calhoun said. Then he jerked his right knee up. It connected with Sculley's groin.

Sculley's eyes widened and he sucked in a breath. He slumped forward, coming to rest against Calhoun, who shoved him to the side. The corporal fell.

"You boys want some?" Calhoun asked the other two corporals.

Neither said anything, but a moment later both charged.

Calhoun moved two paces to his left, stepping on Sculley's head in the process. He swung the corked whiskey bottle, still held in his left hand, up over his right shoulder and then brought the half-empty container down on the back of one corporal's head. The running soldier's impetus made him slam his forehead into the wall. He sank down with a moan, either unconscious or near to it.

Calhoun swung around, leaving his back to the room. That was discomfiting, but he had taken stock of the soldiers before, and none appeared to be overly fond of either Sculley or his two friends. Calhoun figured he was reasonably safe from danger.

The third soldier had slammed on his brakes and stopped before hitting the wall. He spun, set for another run at Calhoun. But Calhoun had a Dragoon in hand. The corporal stopped, half bent over. He was filled with anger, and wariness.

Sculley had managed to get up, bringing out his pistol as he did so. His face was pasty white with the pain of his mashed genitals. "Son of a bitch bastard," he lisped, raising his pistol.

Calhoun swung his revolver barrel a little to his right and calmly fired twice. The two slugs to his chest drove Sculley back against the wall, where he slid down, gun falling from his dead fingers.

The third corporal used the distraction to launch himself at Calhoun. Calhoun managed to take a half step to his right and started to spin on his heel. The movement blunted the soldier's force some, and he hit Calhoun with only part of his left shoulder. Calhoun slammed his pistol butt down on the back of the man's head.

The corporal stumbled a few paces and fell. Calhoun stepped back a little, until his back was against a wall. That was so he could cover either of the two corporals, as well as any other soldier who might want to get in on the action. He determined that the second one was still out, so he could concentrate on the third.

The soldier rolled onto his back and clawed for his pistol. Calhoun decided he would not wait for the man to get the weapon out. He fired twice again, one ball breaking the man's left arm just above the elbow. The other punched a hole in his throat.

Calhoun swung back to glance at the unconscious corporal, but he had not moved.

"Drop that piece, mister," a man barked. "Now!"

Calhoun swung that way, pistol ready. A burly, Teutonic-looking sergeant stood there, arms akimbo. Fanning out from him to each side were four privates, their pistols trained on Calhoun.

"I'm not averse to shootink you, despite vot the major vill say. I know you and him are acquaintances. But I vill risk his wrath if you don't come along peacefully." He accent was muted, but noticeable.

Calhoun shrugged and pointed his pistol toward the ceiling. He eased the hammer down. As he lowered his arm he flicked his fingers. When his gun stopped at waist level, the Dragoon's grip was facing the soldiers.

"Dot is goot, *mein herr,*" the sergeant said. "Private O'Hara, take his veapons."

A short, nervous-looking man edged carefully up on Calhoun. He snatched the Dragoon out of Calhoun's hand and tossed it to one of his companions. Calhoun thought he'd say boo to the other young man, just to scare him, but O'Hara looked like the kind who would squeeze the trigger accidentally if startled. Calhoun kept quiet.

Moments later Calhoun's second Dragoon followed the first. O'Hara took Calhoun's knife and walked back to his friends.

"Move, pliss," the sergeant said.

Calhoun shrugged again and did as he was told. He stopped, as ordered, at the door, and heard the noncom say, "Privates Villiams and Kohl, you vill escort Corporal Jordan to the hospital. Some of you others vill bring the dead vones to the undertaker's."

Once he saw that he was being obeyed, he turned back to Calhoun. "Move, Mr. Calhoun. You know vhere the guardhouse is."

Calhoun walked outside into the soft, gentle night. It was far too nice out, he thought, for all the blood that had been shed in the past few moments. He turned and marched across the parade grounds toward the small stone guardhouse. He had spent more than a little time in it years ago, when he was working fairly regularly for Mangum. He had been younger then, and he and the soldiers were known to have a little too much ruckus juice and get into a brawl.

Inside the guardhouse, Calhoun was relieved of his gun belt and was placed in a cell that was locked behind him. The sergeant and three privates left, leaving only one behind as a guard. He had the front part of the building for an office and quarters. The back of the building housed four cells. The only partition between them were the iron bars. Two men occupied the cell diagonally across from Calhoun. The other two each held one man. All were soldiers, and they looked dispassionately at Calhoun.

Calhoun stretched out on the iron bunk that had only one thin blanket as a covering. He folded his arms behind his head and stared up at the ceiling. He couldn't believe how foolish the soldiers had been in not searching him. Not only did they miss his dagger, which he had taken to wearing down in his boot, they also missed his backup gun. Nestled in a special holster at the small of his back was a Colt Walker with the barrel cut down to about two inches. He had more than fifty grains of powder in each of the five cylinders he kept loaded. With that much powder in them, the lead balls had barely enough room to fit. It was a devastating weapon at close range, and more than once it had saved Calhoun's life.

He figured he could use the pistol after a while, but he decided to wait and see what happened. Major Miles Mangum was not a man to act rashly, and it had to be common knowledge that Sculley and his two friends were braggarts and bullies who had simply met justice. Still, Mangum might be constrained by his military rule book.

Calhoun's biggest regret at the moment was in missing out on Naomi's tender ministrations. Damn, he thought, she had been good. Good for him, too.

Calhoun shut out those thoughts as too pleasant in such a dismal place, though he knew things could be a lot worse. Under the building was a dungeon, where the most incorrigible prisoners were kept. It was a severe punishment, as there was only a fraction of light four times a day—when the flap at the bottom of the door was opened at each of the two mealtimes, just long enough to slide a bowl of food, a cup of water, and a spoon inside, and again an hour later when the dishes were collected.

Calhoun also tried to blot out the thoughts of his wife and daughter, so long dead. It was not easy, but he finally managed. Sleep came then.

Wallace came to visit him the next morning, just after the other prisoners were released, having served their terms. Wallace stood outside the cell. He shook his head at the way Calhoun was being treated. "It ain't fair, dammit, not fair at all," he noted.

Calhoun shrugged. "Fair or not, here I am, and here's where I'm gonna be for a spell," he said philosophically.

"Bah," Wallace spat. He looked at Calhoun and grinned a little. "Naomi missed you last night," he said.

"What do you know about it?"

"I know a lot of things," Wallace said cryptically.

Calhoun looked closely at Wallace. Something about him seemed mighty familiar—more familiar than just a nodding acquaintance with the man. Suddenly something clicked in his head. "You're her father, ain't you?" he asked, surprised, though he didn't know why.

Wallace nodded. He seemed sad. "Ruby's her mother," he said a little defensively. "She's been a good woman all these years. It's why I never sold her—or gave her her freedom, though she's certainly earned it."

Calhoun kept quiet, letting Wallace talk. "But, hell, I don't know what to do about Naomi. She needs a husband, but I can't let her go with any of the men here. They'd only abuse her somethin' awful."

He paused, then sighed. "I think I sorta hoped you and her . . . well, you . . ." He stopped again. "Dammit, I know that ain't gonna happen." He half grinned. "Well, at least she knows now there's good men around, besides her pa."

"You'll find her someone," Calhoun said lamely. He was irritated that Wallace would even think that he wanted to be tied down to another woman after what had happened to Lizbeth. Still, he could understand the man wanting to try.

"I know," Wallace said absentmindedly. He shook off the gloom. "There anything I can do for you, Wade?"

"Reckon not."

"I spoke to the major soon's I heard."

"Obliged."

"I expect you'll get off fairly light, since most of the men had no likin' for Sculley. When you do, stop by the store. Supplies're on me." He grinned a little. "Stop by the house a spell, too," he added.

"I'll be certain of it."

Wallace left. Soon after, a soldier brought Calhoun his breakfast. The fresh bread, bacon, and eggs were a lot better fare than he was used to, and he ate greedily. When he finished, he wiped his lips on his blanket. "Hey, Private," he called. The soldier turned and looked balefully at him.

Calhoun held up his cigarette fixings. "These all right?"

The soldier nodded and went back to his own breakfast.

Calhoun leaned back against the solid back wall of the cell. He savored his coffee and the cigarette. He was almost finished with both when the German sergeant and four privates arrived. The private on duty leaped up and stood at attention. "May I help you, Sergeant?" he asked.

"The major vants to see him." He pointed at Calhoun.

CHAPTER

* 6 *

"You and your men wait outside, Sergeant," Mangum said. When they were gone, Mangum looked at Calhoun. "Stupid bastard," he muttered.

"He seems competent enough to me," Calhoun commented wryly.

"Who?" Mangum asked, surprised.

Calhoun chucked a thumb over his shoulder.

"Sergeant Krumpp?" Mangum said. "Of course he's competent. I was talking about you, though, you dumb son of a bitch."

Calhoun shrugged and sat, this time properly. Mangum handed him a cigar and placed a mug of coffee in front of him.

As he sat Mangum sighed. "What the hell am I going to do with you, Calhoun?" He struck a match on the desk and lit his cigar, then leaned over, holding the flame out to Calhoun, who nodded and sat back once the cigar was going.

"Could let me go," Calhoun said.

"I ought to," Mangum said. "Sculley and Corporal Blankenship were first-rate idiots. Chickenshit bullies."

Calhoun nodded. "I got that impression."

"Yes, you would." Mangum paused, watching a tendril of cigar smoke corkscrew toward the ceiling. "The other one, Corporal Schmidt, is as bad as the other two."

"How is he?" Calhoun asked evenly.

"Alive, but suffering considerably."

Calhoun shrugged. "I must be losin' my touch."

Mangum shot Calhoun a look of annoyance. He puffed for some minutes, listening to the sounds of the fort coming through the open window: shouted orders, horses snorting and whinnying, mules braying, the clang of a blacksmith's hammer, more.

"We have a problem here, Wade," Mangum finally said. "I can't let you just waltz out of here after killing two of our country's protectors." There was considerable irony in his voice. "On the other hand, I'm not of a mind to hang somebody who simply eradicated some two-legged vermin. It places me in a difficult position."

Miles Mangum was about the closest thing to a friend Calhoun had, though even Mangum was not that close to him. Still, he suddenly felt poorly for having put Mangum in such a dilemma. It wasn't the first time his rash actions and temper had caused trouble for others. Really troublesome, though, was the knowledge that it wouldn't be the last time either.

"I've thought about this considerably, Wade," Mangum continued after some more deliberation.

"And?" The coffee and cigar suddenly tasted unpleasant.

"The army's got plenty of rules, Wade, as you well know." Calhoun nodded, and Mangum continued:

"I've got to abide by them." He smiled just a little. "However, much of following those rules is in how one interprets them. There might be some leeway in interpreting the rules covering this situation considering that you're a civilian."

Mangum sipped some coffee. "But if I'm to do anything to help you, you've got to be some less hardheaded than you usually are. Think you can do that?"

Calhoun shrugged. "Depends."

"Dammit, Calhoun," Mangum snapped. "I'm trying to help you here."

"What've you got in mind?" Calhoun asked.

"Take the job I offered you yesterday," Mangum said flatly.

"I'd rather hang."

"That the way you want to go out?" Mangum demanded harshly. "You want to be known as some goddamn coward who got hanged over two stupid ruffians?"

"If it means not having to deal with some goddamn Sioux, I do," Calhoun offered, his voice just as hard as Mangum's.

"So be it," Mangum said. "Finish your cigar and coffee. I can allow you that much. Then you go back to your cell. I'll set trial for tomorrow. I expect the hanging'll be the day after." He looked troubled, but resolute.

Calhoun nodded. The end was near, he figured, but he didn't feel nearly as relieved as he thought he would. It was, he thought, that damned inexorable will to survive that was so far down that he could not exorcise it, no matter how he tried.

Mangum could see the emotions flickering across Calhoun's normally stoic face. He decided to try once more to get through to his former scout. "You know, don't you, that if you're hanged here, you're going to be buried here, back by the garbage pits?"

Calhoun shrugged. He deserved no better.

"And that means you can't be buried with Lizbeth and Lottie," Mangum said quietly.

Hate, rage, and even fear sparkled in Calhoun's dark eyes as the horror of that swept over him. Since the day he found his family dead and his farmstead in ruins, he had carried with him a neatly folded piece of paper. In his bold, purposeful handwriting, he let it be known that no matter where he was when he died, he was to be brought back to the cemetery in Kansas Territory, where Lizbeth and Lottie were buried. He had paid for the plot, the undertaker's cost, and had enough money put up in a bank to pay for transportation of his body. The undertaker had thought him crazy when he proposed it, but the sight of those two twenty-dollar gold pieces convinced him.

"When do we leave?" he asked, chest tight with the rage.

"Day after tomorrow," Mangum said with a little smile. He had thought it appropriate to offer Calhoun the choice of dying or leaving on the same day. "Spend the time as you wish, as long as you don't leave the fort."

Calhoun nodded, still enraged. Any friendship he might have felt for Mangum was gone. He knew even without having to think about it that after this job was done, he'd come back here and gut Mangum for pulling such a thing on him. He considered killing Mangum now. It would be easy enough with the backup gun he carried. But he knew he'd never make it out alive. Despite what he had said, he did not want to die by hanging. He would much prefer to go to his final reward with guns blazing. He would wait to finish off Major Miles Mangum. First, though, there were practical things to think of.

"I need a horse," he said. "And other supplies."

"Of course. Get what you need from Wallace's store. And go see Noble about a horse." He kept a straight face.

"Old man Noble's still around?" Calhoun asked, face showing his distaste. He could not bear the man, and always thought it ironic that a man could be so misrepresented by his name. Calhoun found the man crude and entirely detestable.

"Yep," Mangum said with a small grin. "Still as pleasant as ever."

"You tell him to have the best horse he's got over at Wallace's house at dawn day after tomorrow," Calhoun said flatly.

"You don't want to pick the animal?" Mangum asked, not surprised. Between Calhoun's luck with horses and his dislike for the wrangler, it made sense.

"Hell, when did you ever know me to be a good judge of horseflesh?" Calhoun countered.

"All right," Mangum said with a small laugh.

"How much're you payin' for this job?"

"Your life," Mangum said, his laughter gone.

"That ain't much," Calhoun said truthfully.

"Reckon so. But that, the horse, and your supplies, it ought to be enough."

"I suppose." He took a drag on the cigar and blew out an almost perfect smoke ring. "Am I free now?" he asked after the ring had dissolved.

Mangum nodded. "Like I said, you can go anywhere you want except leave the fort. You can pretty much do anything you want, too, as long as it doesn't break any rules."

"That eliminates quite a bit."

Mangum shrugged. He called for Sergeant Krumpp. When the noncom entered the office, the major said, "Mr. Calhoun is free. He is to be left alone, unless he does something else to disturb the peace, or if he tries to leave the fort proper."

"Yes, sir," Krumpp said. "Are his veapons to be returned?"

Mangum nodded.

Krumpp saluted and then left. Calhoun followed him out a few minutes later. He was still seething, but had managed to get himself under control. He wandered to the guardhouse, where the private on duty handed him his gun belt and the big bowie knife.

Calhoun slid the knife away. Then he buckled on the belt and checked both Dragoons. They were loaded, but had no caps. He reached into the hard-leather pouch on his gun belt and pulled out a small buckskin bag full of caps. He placed new caps on the nipples of both cap-and-ball Colts.

While Calhoun was doing that the private said quietly,

"There's many a man here thought you done right."

Calhoun nodded. "My pleasure," he said before turning and leaving. He went straight to Wallace's store and recited for the sutler a list of things he would need for the journey. When he finished, he said, "The major says the army's payin' for it all."

Wallace nodded. This would work out well. He could overcharge a little on every item, and the army would not question it this time. "When're you leavin'?" he asked.

"Day after tomorrow." He paused, then asked, "You mind if I stay at your place?"

"Nope," Wallace said eagerly.

"You got some whiskey stashed over there?"

"Nope. But I got some here." He turned and retrieved a bottle. Then he picked up some wheat-straw cigarette papers, a pouch of Bull Durham tobacco, and a box of lucifers. He set them on the table. "Just don't give none of that bug juice to Naomi, eh," he said with a chuckle that rang false.

It was evident to Calhoun that Wallace figured that he and Naomi might become real friendly in the next two days. He wasn't having any of it, though. He nodded, picked up his goods, and left.

Ruby let him in when he knocked on the door of Wallace's house. She was surprised but happy. He explained briefly what had happened. Ruby nodded and led him to the small room.

"You want me to fetch Naomi fo' you, Massah Calhoun?" she asked, smiling.

"I'd be obliged," he said. As Ruby turned to leave, though, he added, "But only if she's willin'."

Ruby looked over her shoulder at him and laughed. "Oh, she be willin', Massah Calhoun. She be real willin'!" Still chuckling, she left. She knew there was no chance of Calhoun and her daughter forming any kind of permanent relationship like she herself had with Wallace. But she thought it important that Naomi learn that there were some decent white men, that not all of them were the slobbering pigs who normally populated the fort.

Naomi knocked on Calhoun's door and stepped in boldly rather than shyly. Not that she thought she was better than she was; just that she felt secure in knowing that Calhoun wanted her. Such a thing emboldened her a little. She felt a moment's unease, though, when she saw Calhoun. He was not smiling, and she thought that perhaps her mother had lied to her, telling her that he wanted her.

Then she saw the desire in his eyes, and she was relieved. She realized then that Calhoun never smiled. It made her feel sorry for him. He was a good man, and had much to give. It was a pitiable thing that he could never enjoy laughter.

Calhoun and Naomi hardly ever stepped foot outside the room that day or the next. About the only time they did was to use the outhouse or to eat. The latter was rather awkward. Wallace felt odd when he allowed Naomi to sit at the table with him and Calhoun and had Ruby and Joshua serve them. Ruby didn't mind, but Joshua seemed surly.

Calhoun saw it, but didn't much care. Let the boy

brood, he figured. Life was tough enough, especially for slaves, without begrudging your sister a little comfort.

On the next night Calhoun spent time checking over his gear. He cleaned and oiled all his weapons, including the backup Walker. The latter he pulled out when Naomi had her back turned a moment. He replaced it the same way. It might be paranoid of him, but he wanted as few people as possible to know about the weapon.

He molded lead balls for his weapons and made sure the extra cylinders for the pistols he carried were ready. Then he sharpened the bowie, running the honing stone smoothly along the blade. He did the same for the dirk he carried in his boot.

Finally he cleaned himself up and winked at Naomi. She grinned and stretched out on the bed, where she had been sitting. In between his times that night with her, Calhoun polished off the bottle of whiskey.

In the morning the two of them had a final time together before going to breakfast. Wallace was not there, but returned a few minutes after Naomi and Calhoun had started eating. He took his seat and started heaping food on his plate.

"A mule's tied outside the house, Wade. It's packed with all you bought yesterday and a few other things I thought you might need. You don't like the way it's packed, I'll have it done over."

"I expect it'll be just fine."

Calhoun was just finishing a second cup of coffee when he heard a knock on the front door. Wallace hurried to get it, then came back. "It's Noble with your horse."

"What's it look like?" Calhoun asked.

"It's got four legs, a head, and a tail." Lester Wallace was no better a judge of horseflesh than Wade Calhoun was.

CHAPTER

7

"Mr. Calhoun," Mangum said, "this is Medicine Bear. He has been chosen by his people to meet with the president's representative."

Calhoun took stock of the warrior. The Sioux was about five-foot-seven and stockily built. His skin was quite dark, and his face dominated by high, prominent cheekbones and a sizable beak of a nose. He wore a long, fringed buckskin shirt, matching leggings, and a breechcloth. Two white eagle feathers fluttered from his long, greasy hair. There was no humor or humanity in his flat, dark eyes. Across his back, diagonally, was a bow case with the bow unstrung and a quiver of arrows. Calhoun could see the warrior's shield on his pony.

Medicine Bear, in turn, took the measure of Calhoun. What he saw was a man of five-foot-ten, slightly built, but strong looking. He was smooth-shaven, though his hair was shaggy and ill-kempt. He had a deadly, unforgiving air about him and a determined set to his lightly pocked face.

Calhoun nodded once, a movement returned by Medicine Bear, then turned back to tightening the cinch of his saddle. The horse he had been given was a gawky-looking thing of indeterminate color, though it seemed to be mostly some shade of brown. He just hoped the animal would last. With the saddle tightened, he turned to Mangum again.

"These are the troopers who'll be traveling with you, Mr. Calhoun," Mangum said. "Sergeant Whitcomb and Private O'Shea, whom I think you know already."

Calhoun nodded at the two men.

Almost as an afterthought, the major pointed to the Indian woman. "Medicine Bear's wife, Painted Sky, and their two sons. The older is Fat Bear, and the little one there"—he pointed—"is Red Arrow."

Calhoun nodded at the woman, figuring the greeting would suffice for her and her children. Painted Sky was, he thought, a lot more attractive than he would have expected. She was shorter than her husband, and somewhat fairer of skin. Her long hair was well greased and hung in two braids down onto her chest. The part of her hair was painted vermilion. Her dress was undecorated, except for fringe along the yoke and hem. She also wore leggings and plain moccasins.

"We best be on our way," Calhoun said. He could feel the rage building up in his breast as he looked at the arrogant Medicine Bear. That anger was blunted only a little by the beauty of Painted Sky and the chubby faces of her children. He pulled himself up onto the horse. He sat waiting while the others mounted.

Sergeant Gerard Whitcomb led the way, followed by Private Ian O'Shea, who held the rope to the mule on which were packed his and Whitcomb's supplies.

Medicine Bear rode next, looking almost regal on his painted pony. He was followed by Painted Sky and Fat Bear, who rode side by side. Fat Bear, a boy of about six, looked nearly as haughty as his father as he rode his small pinto. Behind Painted Sky was a mule with her lodge and supplies on a travois. Behind Fat Bear came another horse with a travois on which two-year-old Red Arrow rode. Bringing up the rear was Calhoun and his mule.

The ride through the Sioux camps outside the fort seemed to take forever. Though Calhoun was uncomfortable with all the red faces staring at his entourage, he did not show it. Finally they were beyond the Sioux lodges and on the prairie.

Calhoun rode slackly more often than not, his eyes half-closed in brooding intensity. A thousand times that first day he saw himself drawing one of the big Walkers from the saddle holster and blasting Medicine Bear into oblivion. He didn't know why he didn't, other than that he had given his word to Mangum that he would take on this job. Pride in a job well done was important to Calhoun. He did not give his word lightly, and when he did, he stuck to it as best he could, no matter what the odds.

Near noon, they spotted a couple of buffalo a quarter of a mile or so away. Whitcomb sent O'Shea out after them. O'Shea rode back, red-faced with embarrassment after succeeding only in driving the buffalo away.

Medicine Bear laughed at O'Shea's incompetence. "Sioux children do better," he said with that arrogant air of his.

"You're so goddamn good, you redskin son of a bitch, you go do it next time," O'Shea snapped.

Calhoun expected Whitcomb to remonstrate with O'Shea and was surprised when the sergeant said nothing.

Soon after, they saw some more buffalo. Medicine Bear pulled out his bow and strung it, then pulled out four arrows. He nocked one loosely and held the other three in his left hand, parallel to the bow. "You watch, you learn," he said. Then he galloped off.

The travelers stopped to watch. Medicine Bear moved swiftly across the rolling land, heading at an angle so he could come up downwind of the buffalo. He disappeared into a coulee. When the others next saw him, he was on the far side of the buffalo. He rode toward one of the shaggy beasts and suddenly screeched. The cow he had chosen jerked her big head up and rumbled off, Medicine Bear driving the animal straight toward those watching.

Twenty-five yards away Medicine Bear pulled alongside the buffalo and in the blink of an eye had put two arrows almost through its body. The beast rumbled on a few more yards and then skidded along on its face, blood pouring out of its nose and mouth. It finally stopped, kicking a little, less than ten yards from where O'Shea sat ashen-faced on his horse.

Medicine Bear unstrung his bow as he walked his horse toward his wife. He jerked his head in the direction of the buffalo. Painted Sky rode there and pulled her knife. With sureness built of long practice, she peeled off some of the hide and laid it to the side. Then she began carving out meat, placing it on the hunk of hide.

Calhoun was of half a mind to go help her, not so much because he was bothered by her doing the work while all the men sat around, but because he was eager to be on the go again. The faster he got these damn Sioux to Fort Kearny, he figured, the better off he would be. Then he could go about his own business again, like taking care of Major Miles Mangum.

Still, he sat there, not wanting to insult Medicine Bear or Painted Sky. There would be enough trouble on the trip without that. He finally pulled out his fixings and rolled a smoke.

Medicine Bear saw it and rode up to face Calhoun, their knees almost touching. "I want tobacco," the Sioux said.

Calhoun pulled the drawstring of the Bull Durham pouch closed with his teeth and dropped it into the pocket of his green-and-white-striped shirt. "Piss off, Chief," he said.

Medicine Bear looked as if he had just been slapped. "You will die, white eyes," he snarled, face twisting up in rage.

"We'll all die someday."

"During our journey you will die," Medicine Bear corrected himself.

Calhoun shrugged as he lit the cigarette. "I promised the major I'd get you to Fort Kearny," he said ominously. "I didn't promise him you'd be alive when I got you there."

Medicine Bear's eyes looked like small coals.

He had been insulted like that by a white man once before. It took the white man two full days and one night to die. And he did not die bravely. Medicine Bear thought it would be interesting to apply the same things to this hard-eyed white man. Then he looked into Calhoun's eyes and the smallest chill ran up his back, for he saw the immense hatred he himself had for white men reflected in Calhoun's eyes. He was not really afraid of the man, but it was almost startling to see his own deep animosity in another's eyes. He thought Calhoun would be a superb warrior. That did not lessen his hatred any.

"Time to move, boy," Calhoun said.

Painted Sky had returned to her place in the line, the buffalo meat wrapped in a bloody hide and tied onto the travois with their supplies.

"We will go when I say," Medicine Bear said indignantly.

"Suit yourself," Calhoun said. He brushed his spurs against the horse's side and moved past Medicine Bear. For a moment Calhoun caught a glimpse of Painted Sky's face. He could have sworn she had smiled just a little at him. Then he shook the notion off, since the very thought was ridiculous.

The warrior hastened to catch up, throwing black looks at Calhoun as he moved past and took his place in the column.

Their noon stop was a short one, designed more to give the animals a rest than the people. Saddles were loosened but not removed, nor were supplies unloaded, other than those needed at the moment.

The horses and mules grazed and drank from the trickle of a stream.

The soldiers broke out some hardtack and washed the crunchy, flat-tasting biscuits down with canteen water. Calhoun opened a tin of peaches and another of tomatoes. He was eating the peaches when he got the notion that someone was staring at him. The feeling was accurate. Both Painted Sky and Fat Bear were watching him with considerable interest. He held out the can. "Want a taste?" he asked.

Painted Sky looked greedily at the can, but was afraid to move, lest her husband take it poorly. She smiled wanly and looked away.

Fat Bear was not so fearful. He strutted up to Calhoun. "Taste," he said.

Medicine Bear snapped at the child in Sioux. Calhoun could not understand the words, but by the tone, he figured the warrior was telling his son to get away from Calhoun. The boy stopped, torn between his desire to try this strange new treat and fear of displeasing his father.

"It's all right, boy," Calhoun said. "Your old man ain't gonna hurt you." He was surprised at his liking for the child. By all looks, this little brat was going to turn into an insufferable, arrogant man just like his father. He decided he didn't need to worry about that right now. He dipped his spoon into the can and fished out a chunk of peach. He held the dripping spoon out.

Fat Bear moved toward the spoon as if he were being pulled. He grabbed the piece of peach and shoved it into his mouth. His eyes lit up at the sweetness of the fruit. "Good," he said.

Calhoun nodded.

"More," Fat Bear said eagerly.

"Come sit, boy," Calhoun said. He shared the rest of the peaches with the youngster. Fat Bear was unaware of his father's growing anger, but Calhoun was not. He kept a watch on Medicine Bear, just in case the warrior wanted to try something.

When the peaches were gone, Fat Bear looked quite sad. "Don't you fret, boy," Calhoun said. "We got us somethin' else to try." He peeled open the can of tomatoes and let the boy try one. Fat Bear made a face and spit the tomato out.

"Don't suit you, eh, boy?" Calhoun said. "Ah, well, we can't all like the same things." He dug into the tomatoes.

"More other," Fat Bear said, struggling with the little English he knew. He picked up the empty peach can.

Calhoun wondered where the boy had learned any English at all. He was certain that Medicine Bear would not speak it, or allow it to be spoken, around his lodge. Calhoun suspected that Medicine Bear knew far more English than he was letting on. It would be just like someone like that to play up to the whites by pretending to be just some ignorant savage, when he really knew plenty of English. He could pick up a lot of information that way from whites too ignorant or blind to see they were being bamboozled.

"I ain't got no more peaches," Calhoun said to the boy.

Fat Bear rose and waddled over to his mother.

Painted Sky had unlaced the thongs of her dress over the left shoulder, baring her breast. She was sitting there breast-feeding Red Arrow.

Calhoun shook his head as he spotted both Whitcomb and O'Shea staring brazenly at Painted Sky's bared breast. He could understand, perhaps, O'Shea doing it, since he was young and most likely had seen little of the world. Whitcomb, on the other hand, was considerably older and should not be so entranced by such a thing.

Calhoun dropped the empty tomato tin and wiped his spoon off on a bandanna. He pushed up and headed toward the horses. As he came up alongside Whitcomb he said quietly, sarcastically, "Ain't you ever seen a bare tit before, Sarge?"

Whitcomb shot him a glance that was at once angry and embarrassed. "I've seen more than my share, boy-o," he said.

"Don't seem like it the way you're sittin' there starin' at that squaw's tit. Hell, you ought to have more pride." He continued his walk to his horse and stuffed the spoon into one of his saddlebags.

He tightened the cinch on his saddle and patted the horse's mane. He had found no flaws in the horse so far, and that was a welcome relief. The horse might be as ugly as a rotting tree, but he seemed to ride well. Calhoun mounted the horse. "Time to move," he said evenly.

Painted Sky pulled the child from her breast and retied her dress. She stood and moved toward the pony with Red Arrow's travois. Fat Bear jumped on his pony, which he was riding bareback, as was his father. Painted Sky had a woman's saddle with a high pommel and almost as high cantle.

Even Medicine Bear stood and made his way lazily toward his pony. He thought a nap would be enjoyable now. It was not good to do much with a full stomach. Still, he knew this white man was not one to be ignored. He fully intended to kill Calhoun, slowly and painfully, but he would wait for the proper time.

"We'll go when I say we go," Whitcomb announced. "And that ain't for a spell yet."

"Stay as long as you like," Calhoun said. "The rest of us are movin' on."

With the Indians all mounted, Calhoun nodded, and Medicine Bear moved off, followed by Painted Sky, the children, and the mules. Calhoun followed them, glancing back occasionally.

Whitcomb and O'Shea had lingered there a few more moments. Then, when they realized that Calhoun had been serious, they jumped up and hurried toward their horses. Within minutes they were loping toward the procession and taking their accustomed spot in the lead.

It was an unhappy group, all in all, that pulled into a campsite along a small stream late that afternoon.

CHAPTER

8

Calhoun moved off a few yards from the others. He hated the Indians—at least the warrior; he was no longer sure that he hated Painted Sky or the two children—and he wanted to be away from them. He was not too fond of the soldiers at the moment, either, and wanted to keep his distance from Whitcomb and O'Shea.

He unsaddled the splotchy horse and pulled off the bridle. He began wiping down the animal with a worn brush. "Goddamn, you're an ugly old thing, ain't you," he muttered. Then he shook his head. "At least you're alive."

When he finished that, he unloaded the mule and gave that animal a cursory grooming. Finally he went about finding wood for a fire. Though he hated cooking for himself, he wanted no part of supping with either the Indians or the two soldiers.

With a fire going and some salt beef cooking and coffee boiling, Calhoun sat on an old log and rolled a cigarette. He was partially shaded from the others by a screen of thorny brush and tall weeds. The creek bank to his left stank of stagnant water, damp, ripe mud, and dying vegetation.

While he waited for his supper he stared balefully

through the foliage at the others. Painted Sky had unsaddled her horse, unloaded the two travois, and put up their lodge. She was just getting around to gathering firewood. Calhoun was a little surprised to note that the woman was rather pigeon-toed.

All the while that Painted Sky worked, an imperious Medicine Bear sat cross-legged where he wanted his lodge to be. Six-year-old Fat Bear sat next to him, looking for all the world like a miniature version of his haughty father. Two-year-old Red Arrow tottered around, exploring.

Calhoun shook his head. He wished he had a woman around to do most of the mundane work, but he figured he would at least give her some help, even if only caring for the animals. He sighed. This was the Sioux way, he supposed; had been for centuries. It was not going to change now.

Of more annoying interest were the two soldiers. They, too, sat there watching the woman. Even from his position some yards away through the brush, Calhoun could see that they were not looking at her with innocent interest. Sergeant Whitcomb had done nothing at all since arriving. Private O'Shea had cared for both horses and unloaded the mule before going to sit beside Whitcomb. They passed a small bottle of whiskey between them.

Dark was coming fast. Calhoun flicked his cigarette butt into the small fire and pulled the pan out. He stabbed the hunk of meat with his bowie knife and hoisted it. He held the meat up and gnawed off pieces. He wished he had some of the buffalo that Painted Sky was just beginning to cook, but the Sioux had not offered him any. He was not about to ask for it. Nor would he sit there silently begging, as the soldiers were doing. They seemed to think that Painted Sky would cook for them as well as her family.

Calhoun was done eating long before the others even started, and he sat sipping a mug of coffee and smoking. He moved away from the fire a little so he could not be seen, other than by the moving, glowing tip of his cigarette. He could catch glimpses of the others in the flickering firelight.

Ghostly scraps of conversation drifted his way on the night breeze, almost all of it from Whitcomb and O'Shea. The two troopers were not drunk, but the whiskey had lowered their inhibitions some, and so their crude comments directed at the Sioux, especially Painted Sky, grew more boisterous and crude.

Calhoun caught a glance of the whiskey bottle gleaming in the firelight as Whitcomb drained it. Then the sergeant flung the bottle into the darkness, right at Calhoun.

Calhoun lost sight of the bottle in the darkness, but then his fire showed it. He just managed to duck his head out of the way and shoot a hand up and out. He caught the bottle, surprised at his own luck. He held it a moment, looking at it. Then something of a grin—a devilish rather than a humorous one—crossed his lips. He flipped the bottle and then caught it again, this time by the short neck. He threw it.

He almost smiled for real when the bottle clanked off O'Shea's head and bounced into the dirt.

"Son of a bitch," O'Shea cursed, and reached up to touch his head.

"Goddammit, Calhoun, watch what you're doin'," Whitcomb shouted.

"Piss off," Calhoun said with what for him was a touch of joviality. He finished his cigarette and then spread out his bedroll. Tossing his hat aside, he lay face up, conscious of the cut-down Walker at the small of his back. He folded his hands up behind his head and fell asleep, the sounds of the soldiers demanding buffalo meat from the Sioux ringing in his ears. Calhoun half expected to wake up to find either the soldiers or Medicine Bear dead.

All were alive, though the two soldiers didn't look very enthusiastic. Calhoun figured they were suffering hangovers. They gingerly poured themselves coffee and sat back to drink it.

Calhoun cooked up some bacon and pancakes and ate heartily. Afterward he bolted down another cup of coffee, then cleaned up. It did not take long to load the panniers on his mule, and saddle and bridle his horse. He looked over toward the others.

Painted Sky was breaking down the tipi—alone, of course—trying to ignore the soldiers' crude entreaties for her to serve them. Finally Whitcomb ordered O'Shea to cook some of the buffalo meat. O'Shea wanted to argue, but couldn't.

Calhoun sat back on his log to wait. He might want to hurry Whitcomb and O'Shea, but he could not push Painted Sky. The woman was working as fast as she could and was getting no help. Calhoun considered aiding her to move things along some, but he was fairly certain that Medicine Bear would not look too kindly on such a thing. Not that he cared what Medicine Bear thought, but he did not want the Sioux taking it out on Painted Sky.

That worried Calhoun. He hated Indians, and these he was traveling with were the worst of the lot. Yet he found himself looking somewhat favorably on Painted Sky. While she was attractive and had an earthy sensuality about her, he did not—could not—like her. The very thought was ridiculous. He told himself silently that he cared about what happened to her simply because she was a woman, and he hated to see any woman abused.

Another factor, he realized, was that he found he couldn't hate Indian women quite as much as he did Sioux warriors. After all, there had been no women in that war party that descended on his farmstead while he was off on some job.

"Ah, the hell with it all," he growled quietly. He tried to put it all out of his mind, succeeding for the most part.

When Painted Sky was finished packing her things, Calhoun rose and walked his horse and mule toward the main campfire. "Time to move," he said quietly. He looked at Medicine Bear, both men glaring for a moment in their mutual hatred. Then the Indian nodded. He could hate this pale-skinned man and still understand that it was time to leave. He would lose no face in agreeing.

"We ain't done," Whitcomb barked.

Calhoun shrugged. "You hurry, you can catch us." He pulled himself onto the horse. "You first, Chief," he said.

Medicine Bear glared at him again, but then moved on, leading the procession out of the campsite.

Calhoun brought up the rear, watching over his shoulder in case either trooper attempted something. They still sat there, though, as if not believing this was happening. Just before a small, grassy knob obscured the men from view, Calhoun saw the two soldiers jump up and trot to their horses.

Calhoun continued to keep a lookout behind him. It was still quite possible that Whitcomb, O'Shea, or both would try something. They could not be happy at their treatment, particularly Whitcomb. Being a sergeant, he was used to giving orders. Of course, he was used to taking them, too, though not from a civilian.

Almost an hour later the soldiers galloped up, their horses foamed with sweat from the hard run in the heat. As they passed Calhoun, Whitcomb shot him a hateful look. Calhoun shrugged, annoying the sergeant all the more. The two soldiers took their positions at the lead and rode stiff-backed with anger.

Once again the noon stop was brief. When they were on the move again, Calhoun quietly dropped back and then turned north. He was sure the Sioux had seen him, but he didn't figure Whitcomb and O'Shea had. Minutes later he found a few grazing buffalo. He dropped a big cow with a shot from his Henry rifle. The other bison scattered.

He rode up and dismounted near the buffalo. The horse seemed skittish around the fresh blood, so Calhoun walked it and the mule a few feet away, where he pounded a picket ring into the ground and tied the two animals to it.

He reloaded his rifle and then leaned it against the buffalo's head and began butchering. With his sharp bowie and years of experience, it did not take Calhoun long to carve out the tongue, hump meat, and some ribs. He placed the meat on a piece of hide, as Painted Sky had done the day before, wrapped it up, and tied it with a rawhide thong.

It took almost as long to pack the meat on the mule as it had to butcher it. The mule's load had to be rearranged and some of the supplies dropped in a bag hanging from the saddle on the horse. Only then could he hoist the bloody package onto the mule.

He trotted back toward the small column, taking his place at the rear. Whitcomb looked back angrily, and Calhoun made an obscene gesture at him.

By late afternoon they pulled into a wooded stretch along the Platte River. As was his wont, Calhoun moved off to be by himself. He cared for his animals and made his small camp. After gathering firewood and cleaning up a little in the sluggishly moving river, he opened the hide filled with meat. He pulled out the tongue and a couple of ribs. He rolled the hide back up and hefted it. He walked to where Painted Sky had just finished putting up her lodge. Calhoun handed her the hide-wrapped meat.

"Make sure you give some to those two damn fools," Calhoun said, nodding in the direction of

Whitcomb and O'Shea, "lest they starve to death." He had no idea of whether the woman could understand him. She had never said anything in English within Calhoun's hearing, but that did not mean she didn't understand it or speak it.

Painted Sky nodded, the grateful look in her soft brown eyes saying far more than the nod. Calhoun now knew that she at least understood English. Not that it mattered much, he thought as he walked back to his little camp.

He wondered about the woman. She seemed interested in him, but, he thought, perhaps he was reading more into a few grateful looks cast his way than was really meant. He built his fire up and began making coffee and roasting the buffalo meat.

As he had the night before, he sat smoking a cigarette and watched the others as his supper cooked. The tableau before him was little changed from that of the previous night, except that the soldiers were not drinking.

After riding for two full days with the soldiers, little Red Arrow had lost much of his fear of these strange hairy men. Not only did they look strange, but they smelled funny to him, too. He just had to see close up if they were real.

As his mother was kindling a fire, Red Arrow tottered toward the soldiers, who were sitting on the riverbank a little higher than the others. It took a little doing for the youngster to make his way up there, but he finally succeeded. Creeping along on tiptoe as best as he could, Red Arrow inched up to Whitcomb. The sergeant was busy watching Painted

Sky as she worked, and so was unaware of the child's approach.

Red Arrow reached out a tiny hand tentatively. Then he touched the thick fuzziness on Whitcomb's cheek.

"What the hell?" Whitcomb shouted, half rising, hand heading toward the holstered Colt. Then he saw a wide-eyed, terrified Red Arrow. "You little bastard," he snarled. He slapped the little boy in the face.

Red Arrow made no sound as he rolled down the slight embankment. His mother, though, screeched in anger, and leaped over the fire to stop Red Arrow before he rolled into the flames.

Medicine Bear was on his feet, face calm but eyes snapping with anger. He reached for his bow. Whitcomb saw what the Indian was doing. He snapped his holster open and jerked his revolver out.

Medicine Bear froze, looking at the pistol-wielding soldier. He knew he was dead if he reached for an arrow, now that he had his bow strung.

"Come on, boy," Whitcomb said harshly. "Come on and do it." He sounded eager despite his fear. He thumbed back the hammer, preparing to shoot the Indian anyway.

"Drop the piece, Sarge," Calhoun said as his own Dragoon brushed up against the hair on the back of Whitcomb's head.

"I didn't know you was an Injun lover, Calhoun," Whitcomb said, sweat coating his face.

"I ain't."

"Then why?"

"It ain't right is why. Neither is swattin' a little young'un like that."

"But, goddammit . . ." Whitcomb began.

"No buts, Sarge."

"You wouldn't kill me over slapping some Injun brat, would you?" Whitcomb didn't believe any white man would do that.

"Probably not, though I can't say for sure."

"You stupid son of a bitch," Whitcomb said, rage overtaking him.

Calhoun pulled his pistol away from Whitcomb's head, swung it up over his left shoulder, and than lashed out with it. The barrel cracked into Whitcomb's head a fraction above the ear.

Whitcomb groaned and his knees buckled, but he managed to catch himself before falling.

"Mind how you talk to me, boy." Calhoun paused a moment. "I promised Mangum I'd deliver that son of a bitch to Fort Kearny. I didn't promise anything of the sort about you." He turned and walked away, sliding his pistol into the holster.

CHAPTER

9

A shaky truce sprang up between all the parties the next day. Whitcomb's head was wrapped in a dirty sleeve torn from an old shirt. When he tossed the filthy rag away two days later, the side of his head was still splotchy with a yellowish-purple bruise. Calhoun had no sympathy for him.

He did, however, have some sympathy for Painted Sky. When she stepped out of the lodge the next morning, she kept her face down, not looking at anyone. Even so, Calhoun could see the marks of a beating on her.

Angrily he squatted at his fire and made his breakfast. He didn't know why he was so bothered by having seen that Painted Sky had been beaten. Part of it was that he hated to see any woman so abused. Another part was that he hated Medicine Bear, and so everything bad that the Sioux warrior did was exaggerated in his eyes. Still another thing, though, was that he found himself drawn to the woman. It was not love, but it was more than simple lust, too.

With a sigh, he began eating. Horses and women, he thought. All he had with either was bad luck. *Maybe I ought to give 'em both up,* he thought regretfully. It was not a serious thought, though, since he was unwilling, and unable, to give up either.

Calhoun wondered why Medicine Bear had beaten Painted Sky, though he reasoned that it was probably because of the previous evening's episode with Whitcomb and the child. This made him hate Medicine Bear all the more. The more he thought about it, the more enraged he became. He wasn't sure why, but he didn't care that he didn't know. It was sufficient that he felt that way. The thoughts didn't do much for his digestion, however.

He saw Medicine Bear head into the bushes a little way off. Without really thinking about what he was going to do, Calhoun stood and circled the camp, heading for where he had last seen Medicine Bear. The Sioux's grunting alerted him to where he was. Calhoun stood behind a tree on the path leading back to the camp. He was sure Medicine Bear would have to return this way. The Indian did not look to be the kind of man who would take the difficult way through the brambles and such when there was an easy path to use.

As Medicine Bear was just about to the tree, Calhoun stepped out from behind it, one of his pistols out. He shoved the cocked weapon to within an inch of the Sioux's face, just above the nose. "You ever beat Painted Sky again while I'm around, I'll put a slug into your head, boy."

Medicine Bear stared arrogantly at Calhoun. "You want her, you take her," he said calmly.

"Didn't say I wanted her, Chief. I just said for you to leave off beatin' her."

"She's my woman," Medicine Bear said. "I treat her good."

"Buffalo shit. Just mind my words."

"I'll kill you, goddammit," Medicine Bear said, revealing a much better command of English than he normally allowed himself to do.

Calhoun's eyes burned with the rage that he had planted, cultivated, and carefully reared. "You get your business done at Fort Kearny, and then you come against me, boy," he said, his voice raspy with anger.

Medicine Bear nodded. "I'll let you live till then."

"Big of you," Calhoun said sarcastically, but he was fairly certain he could trust the warrior not to come against him until after the business at Fort Kearny was concluded. "I'll let you live, too—unless you beat on Painted Sky again."

Medicine Bear nodded again.

Calhoun eased down the Dragoon's hammer and slid the weapon away. He turned and walked off, cutting through some brush to keep away from the camp. He reached his own fire and poured himself another cup of coffee.

Life gets too goddamn complicated sometimes, he thought ironically as he rolled a smoke.

It was a thoroughly disgruntled group that rode out that morning. No one spoke unless it was necessary. Gradually, though, Whitcomb and O'Shea began speaking to each other.

Still, it took the Pawnees to bring the group together. They were all plodding along, half-asleep as they rode under the broiling sun. Calhoun shook himself out of his lethargy as he got the impression that he was being followed. For the next half hour or so he frequently looked back over his shoulder, both ways. Suddenly he pulled one of the Walkers from a saddle holster and fired in the air.

In the lead, Whitcomb stopped. He stood in his stirrups and looked behind him. "What the hell . . .?" he began.

Calhoun pointed the Walker over his right shoulder. Whitcomb followed the path, and his eyes widened. Suddenly he was a sergeant in the United States Army, Mounted Infantry. He took a quick look around. There was no cover of any kind nearby. They would have to make a stand here, he reasoned. He started barking orders that only O'Shea followed.

Calhoun had stopped and slid out of the saddle, big Colt Walker still in his right fist. He wrapped the reins up in his left hand. He figured the horse had been well trained, since it had not flinched when he had fired his warning shot.

Damn, here goes another horse, Calhoun thought wryly as he leveled his right hand on the saddle.

Suddenly Medicine Bear was standing a few feet away, his bow strung and nocked.

"You ought to stand watch over your family," Calhoun said heatedly.

"No," Medicine Bear responded flatly.

Calhoun shrugged. It was not his problem. He glanced back and saw that Painted Sky had stopped and was holding the reins to her pony, the mule carrying her youngest son, and the mule with her supplies. Fat Bear was holding his own pony. His eyes were bright with excitement.

Calhoun turned back to face the enemy. He counted eighteen Pawnees racing toward them.

When the Pawnees were on a ridge about a hundred yards away, Whitcomb and then O'Shea fired their carbines, one after the other. With practiced efficiency, each snapped open the rolling block of his rifle, shoved a paper cartridge into the breech, and slapped the block back into place, shearing off the end of the cartridge. A moment later a cap was in place, and each was ready to fire again.

Calhoun held his fire. The Walker, at almost five pounds, was a big and powerful weapon, but only at short distances. Over fifty yards, it was almost useless. He could not see wasting ammunition.

The Pawnees disappeared for a few moments in another hollow and then topped a second ridge. Whitcomb and O'Shea each fired again. Between their two shots each, one Pawnee went down, and one looked as if he might've been hit. As he was reloading, Sergeant Whitcomb looked over at Calhoun. "Shoot, goddammit! What the hell're you waitin' for?"

Calhoun ignored the noncom. When the Pawnees had dipped and then rode up over the ridge about twenty-five yards or so away, he began firing, evenly snapping off the four rounds left in the Walker.

Pawnees began falling, and Calhoun realized that there were a lot more of them than could be accounted for with his firing. He risked a glance to his left as he dropped the empty Walker and grabbed the second. Medicine Bear was firing arrows with deadly accuracy and a lot of force. Calhoun thought it quite ironic that he was standing here with a hated Sioux warrior fighting off another tribe of Indians. He turned back to the battle.

The Pawnees had drawn up sharply about ten yards away and swung around. Now they were racing off, leaving their dead and wounded where they lay.

Medicine Bear swept onto his pony in one easy bound. He kicked the horse into a dead run.

"Where the hell's he goin'?" O'Shea asked no one in particular.

Calhoun shrugged. He had no idea, and so didn't think the question required an answer. He did, however, figure that Medicine Bear was crazy enough to go after the remaining Pawnees by himself. That seemed not only crazy, but strange, too, since Calhoun was sure the Pawnees would be back. Medicine Bear would have to know that. Calhoun had the sudden thought that maybe the Sioux wanted to get some scalps.

Medicine Bear stopped by one of the bodies and slipped off his horse. Watching, Calhoun thought he had the man's reason pegged. It had to be scalps.

He was rather surprised when the Sioux began pulling arrows out of Pawnees bodies. Calhoun supposed he should not be surprised. It only made sense. Arrows were hard to make, and replacing them on a journey like this would be next to impossible.

Medicine Bear was moving fast, and he had gathered almost all his arrows when the Pawnees boiled up over the ridge again. Medicine Bear, on the

Pawnees' right flank, simply spun and knelt. He calmly fired arrows. Three Pawnees swung their ponies in his direction. Moments later all three were dead, punctured by the swift, silent arrows from the Sioux warrior.

Calhoun, who kept watching during the short respite, stuck the empty Walker into this belt and scooped up the other Walker. He brushed the dirt off it and popped out the cylinder. He dropped that into one of his saddlebags and pulled out a loaded replacement. He stuck that one in his belt and went through the ritual with the other Colt Walker. He did it all in moments, while never really taking his eyes off the battlefield.

Then the Pawnees were coming at them again, and Calhoun began firing once more. This time, when the surviving Pawnees turned and rode off, they grabbed as many of their dead and dying as they could. Calhoun watched as the Indians topped the second ridge, and moments later the third one more than a hundred yards off.

Out on the battlefield, Medicine Bear howled in victory. He shouted at the fleeing Pawnees. Calhoun couldn't understand the words, but it was clear that the man was insulting the Pawnees. Then Medicine Bear walked around the battlefield, yanking his arrows free. Among the warriors left behind by the Pawnees were the three who had targeted the Sioux. Medicine Bear went about and scalped them, bringing the three bloody things with him as he rode slowly back to the others. He held the scalps out and whooped.

Calhoun shook his head. He could never understand a man's desire to take scalps, especially the
odd roached ones of the Pawnees. Nor could he
understand why a man would want to decorate his
home with the things once they were cured. Then he
shrugged as he reloaded his two Walkers. It wasn't
his concern. He was not about to tell someone, especially a Sioux, that he was living the wrong way.

Finished loading his pistols, Calhoun returned
them to his saddle holsters and closed the flaps.
Then he walked around, making sure everyone was
all right. They were, and within minutes they were
all mounted and riding on.

For quite a while Calhoun kept a lookout on their
back trail, just to make sure the Pawnees did not
decide to make another run at them. An hour later he
decided it was unlikely that they would come back.

He swung off, heading north, to take a look to
make sure the Pawnees were truly gone, but also to
find some meat. With four men, a woman, and two
children, the small amount of meat they could
afford to pack did not last long. And with this heat
and little time, they could not preserve the meat in
any way.

It did not take long before he jumped a herd of
antelope. The small, wiry animals bounded off, but
by then, Calhoun was off his horse, rifle in hand. He
dropped to one knee, tracked one antelope, and
fired. He caught the animal in midjump. Rather than
wasting the time with the butchering now, he just
threw the carcass over the back of the mule and
rode back to the others.

When they finally made camp on a splotchy island in the shallow Platte, the tension was considerably less than it had been, as the members of the expedition basked in the afterglow of their victory over the Pawnees. That and the different meat for a change created almost a feeling of camaraderie, albeit a fragile one.

When they pulled out in the morning, the shallow goodwill lingered, which was something of a surprise to Calhoun. He did not think it would last the afternoon yesterday, let alone almost a full day.

Gathering storm clouds to the west were worrisome to Calhoun. He hoped that the storm, when it came, would not be a long one or a bad one. Having this group deal with that on top of everything else they had endured would almost guarantee that they would lose whatever fragment of friendship they had found.

Calhoun's hopes were not to be realized, though. The storm hit before they were gone from their last campsite two hours. And when it came, it slammed at them with a fury that was devilish in its intensity. Calhoun had pulled on his slicker at the first sign of rain, and so was as comfortable as could be expected under the situation.

Whitcomb and O'Shea also had slickers, but Medicine Bear and his family did not. However, when the rain started, Painted Sky hurriedly dismounted and grabbed Red Arrow from the travois. She remounted and held the boy in front of her. She draped a thick wool blanket over her head and back, and kept it in place over Red Arrow. Medicine Bear had placed a wolf's-fur hat on his head, but otherwise appeared to be ignoring the storm. His son Fat Bear emulated him.

They did not stop for noon this day. They just kept traveling, and doing so at a much slower pace than usual. That would, they hoped, ease the strain on their animals.

Late in the afternoon, or so he judged it to be, Calhoun left his mule with Painted Sky and rode out ahead of the others. It wasn't long before he found a campsite that would offer little in the way of shelter, though it was better than none at all, he figured.

He rode back to the others and led them toward the campsite. It was a dismal group that stopped at Calhoun's command.

CHAPTER

✻ 10 ✻

As Calhoun had thought it would, the pounding of the rain flooded away whatever small bit of camaraderie the group had found after their battle with the Pawnees. Little Red Arrow was crying almost constantly, the two soldiers were bickering, Painted Sky was being overworked, and Medicine Bear was his usual imperious self. Calhoun was annoyed at the lot of them.

Calhoun began setting up his own little camp, such as it was, amid some scrubby, thorny brush. This far back from the muddy riverbank, there was not much cover. But it was better than being swept away by a flood that filled the Platte.

Medicine Bear knew these things, too, and was wise enough to let experience guide him. He ordered Painted Sky to put up their lodge not far from where Calhoun had formed a crude pup tent with a piece of canvas tied between some of the brush.

Whitcomb and O'Shea, though, were having none of that. They went down to the riverbank, under the cover of several cottonwoods. Smirking, they set up their small pup tents. Well, actually, it was O'Shea who did the setting up while the sergeant sat on a log under a tree directing him.

Calhoun paid them little heed as he cared for his two animals. Finally he spread out his bedroll—two blankets with a waterproof piece of canvas—in his little tent. He scrunched into the shelter and pulled off his hat. It was soaked through. He tossed it aside. He lit a cigarette and watched Painted Sky as she struggled on her own to put her tipi up in the midst of the whistling wind. Seeing Medicine Bear standing there oblivious to almost everything made Calhoun's blood boil. Still, he was not one to help out an Indian, even if that Indian was a young woman and more than a little attractive.

"Hey, Medicine Bear," Calhoun yelled over the wind, thunder, and downpour. The Sioux did not look his way, but that did not deter Calhoun. "Why don't you get off your lazy ass and help your woman?" He was curious, but more than that, he wanted to irritate Medicine Bear some.

Medicine Bear still did not acknowledge him.

"You are one dumb shit, you know that," Calhoun tried again. When that drew no response, he shook his head and shouted, "Dumb bastard'd rather drown than give his old lady a hand. Christ."

Calhoun gave it up then. He was not a man of many words in the first place. Nor was he one to sit there and talk just to hear himself. Besides, he was irked enough already, what with the poor weather, knowing he was going to have a cold supper and probably breakfast, too, having to deal with dimwits like Whitcomb and O'Shea, and with arrogant bastards like Medicine Bear. He felt caged in his tiny shelter.

Sighing, he pulled open his food sack. With a look

of distaste, he grabbed some strips of jerky and gnawed on them with little enthusiasm. Canteen water put the final dull touches on a lousy meal. As he rolled and lit a cigarette he watched Medicine Bear finally enter his lodge, leaving Painted Sky outside to deal with the horses and children, unload the supplies, find firewood, and then cook. "Shit," he muttered under his breath.

Painted Sky put the children inside the tipi. When she stepped outside again, she paused, letting her weariness gain the upper hand a moment. Even in the dying gray light of the miserable day, Calhoun could see her exhaustion. Looking at her, he felt something more than simple sympathy. An instant later that small spark was extinguished. He could not afford even that dim flicker of feeling. She was, after all, a Sioux.

Painted Sky squared her shoulders and pulled the blanket more tightly around her. Then she moved off, looking small and frail.

Calhoun watched her until she was swallowed by the darkness and curtain of rain. He rolled another cigarette. He hated this kind of weather. The desert was hot and a man could easily die from thirst, and maybe even from the baking heat itself. The mountains had clear, thin air that made a man feel funny in the head, and the blizzards there were deadly. The plains were swept by winds all the time, sometimes great gusts or whirling dervishes that could suck a man up and spit his shattered body out miles away. All of them were far deadlier than this thunderous rain, but he hated this weather. There was no explanation for it; he simply detested it.

He flicked the cigarette out into the sheets of rain. It was out before it hit the ground. He slapped his soaking hat on his head, more from habit than from any belief that it might do him some good. Then he stepped out into the rain.

He walked through the deepening darkness, not sure of where he was going or why. It was more than an impulse, though he did not know for sure if it was a hunch. Something pulled him, and he allowed himself to be drawn along.

Dimly, through the roaring of the rain, he thought he heard a muffled voice. Senses alert, he swung to his left a little and proceeded cautiously. He stopped every few feet and listened, hoping to hear something besides the swirling winds, the crack and pop of thunder, the pummeling rain, and the creaking of trees and vegetation.

He heard it again, and he homed in on the sound, instinctively, it seemed. Suddenly a giant shadowy figure loomed just ahead. Calhoun stopped, wondering what he was seeing.

Moments later the shadowy thing split vertically in two, revealing it to be not some monster of the night, but two people. One was fairly tall and slim, the other shorter and rounder of shape.

Calhoun squatted and felt around on the ground, still watching the two people struggling. His fingers finally found a piece of wood. He grasped it and stood, hefting it. The wood was about four inches around and two or three feet long.

Calhoun moved like a phantom, his slicker tails flapping like dancing dust devils. He stopped just behind the taller of the two figures and whacked it a good lick in the back of the head. Private Ian O'Shea went down like a leaking sack of grain.

Painted Sky looked up at Calhoun, resignation but no fear in her eyes, not that Calhoun could see it. She simply waited for this pale-skinned man to do what he would do to her.

All Calhoun saw was the pale blob of her face slightly lighter than the blanket around her head and shoulders, and the gloom that surrounded them both. "You best be on about your work, Painted Sky," Calhoun said quietly, "before Medicine Bear comes lookin' for you."

He tossed his stick away into the rain. Then he bent and grabbed the back of O'Shea's wool blouse and hauled him a few feet away and dropped him again. Calhoun melted into the darkness, not seeing the look of surprise in Painted Sky's eyes, as he had not seen the resignation earlier.

Calhoun stopped just outside his small canvas tent. He looked around, seeing next to nothing. He held out a hand. Even that was almost impossible to see, considering the storm's gloom and the night's blackness.

He scrunched into his shelter and tossed his hat down. He ran a hand through his sopping hair, then flicked the hand, sending out a small spray of water.

As he rolled a cigarette he wished he had never let Major Mangum talk him into this crazy venture. Now that he thought about it, Calhoun felt sure he could have talked—or fought—his way out of the trouble back at Fort Laramie. He had done enough work for Mangum in the past that the major should have offered up some kind words about his character. Plus, considering the kind of men Corporal Sculley and Corporal Blankenship were, there wouldn't have been too many objections to what he had done. Besides, it was all done in self-defense.

Calhoun shrugged. It was too late for any of that, he knew. He had given his word, and Wade Calhoun was not a man to go back on his word, even if it had been coerced out of him. He had been that way all his life, and could see no good coming from his changing it now.

The rain had tapered off a little, though it was still a frog strangler of a downpour. He sensed more than saw that Painted Sky had entered her lodge. Soon after there was a fire going inside the tipi. When that happened, he could see shadows moving inside. He noticed that Painted Sky was cooking. That reminded him of the poor fare he had had not long ago. His stomach gave out a gurgling protest and a noisy demand to have something more filling and palatable sent into it.

"Go to hell," Calhoun growled softly at his stomach. He finished the cigarette and then worked off his slicker. He pulled off his muddy, soaked boots and set them aside. Finally he flipped open the top blankets of his bedroll and slipped in. He pulled the covers back over, and then the slicker, wet side up. He figured he'd be warm enough, and mostly dry. Making a poor pillow of his left arm, he laid his head on it. He was asleep minutes later.

Calhoun had no idea how long he had been asleep when something woke him. He lay there, hand resting on the butt of one of his Dragoons, trying to figure out what it was. In a moment he realized that the wind and rained had died down to almost nothing. It was eerie, though, after the earlier cacophony. He heard a small whimper. Confused, he pushed aside the blankets and sat up.

He heard it again, so he peered around the edge of his tent. Inside the tipi, the firelight still provided a view. He could see Medicine Bear behind Painted Sky, who was on her hands and knees. She was not whimpering for pleasure, that much was evident to Calhoun even from where he was.

Calhoun's hand closed around a Colt and began easing the pistol out of the holster. He burned with blood lust. He could remember only one other time when the desire to draw blood, to butcher another human being, to kill was so strong in him.

The muscles of his jaw and chest were tight, almost choking off his air as he struggled with the rage that pulsed in him. With sheer will, he forced himself to lie back down, though his right hand remained on the pistol grip and his muscles still were rigid.

He vowed then and there that Medicine Bear would not return to his people in the Black Hills. He vowed silently that he would wait outside Fort Kearny until the Sioux came out for the return trek to his homeland. That was when he would kill the warrior, without hesitation, without remorse, and the plans of the United States and anyone else be damned. Medicine Bear would die.

The sounds from the nearby tipi had ended, but it was still some time before Calhoun could relax enough to get back to sleep. It was unusual for him, but he slept fitfully, unable to wash away the pictures of his old farmstead and the two abused, pitiful bodies there.

When next he awoke, it was easy to tell why. A screech split the night air. Calhoun sat up, rubbing the sleep from his eyes. The wind had died down and the rain had stopped, moving on to bedevil someone else. Most of the clouds had fled, too, allowing the moon to spread a thin, silvery light over the camp.

Moments later Whitcomb and O'Shea came running up the slight slope, on the flat top of which Calhoun and Medicine Bear had made their shelters. They stopped at Medicine Bear's lodge.

"Let us in there, goddammit," Whitcomb roared. He reached to pull the flap of the tipi open.

Calhoun went for a pistol, then relaxed. He would not need the weapon, since Medicine Bear had flung open the flap himself and stepped out. He was stark naked, his hair falling in wild tendrils down his back and around his face. In his hand was a nasty-looking war club. He shook the head of the club—two buffalo bull horns opposite each other—at the two soldiers.

"Jesus Almighty," Whitcomb said, seeming to leap backward without making an effort.

Medicine Bear snarled at the two white men and blistered them in Sioux, while continuing to shake the wicked war club at them. The soldiers backed off, making sure they were well away from Medicine Bear's tipi before they turned.

"What the hell happened to you goddamn fools?" Calhoun asked, not all that interested.

"Goddamn river come up on us," Whitcomb said, a mixture of wonder and anger in his voice. "We like to drown before we got out and come runnin' up here."

"So you thought that son of a bitch was gonna let you into his lodge?" Calhoun asked, incredulous.

"Never hurts to try," Whitcomb said defensively.

O'Shea looked even more dopey than usual. "What's wrong with you, boy?" Calhoun asked.

"Me?" O'Shea said. "Well, someone went and whacked me upside the head."

"Who?" Calhoun asked innocently.

"I figure it was that bastard," he said, pointing to the lodge. He more than half suspected it was Calhoun, though he would not say so to his face. He knew for sure it had to be either Medicine Bear or Calhoun. Whitcomb would never do it, O'Shea figured. Or he might, if he was trying to get his hands on that Sioux woman.

"Why? What'd you do to him?"

"Nothin'," O'Shea said hastily. "But who can tell what goes on in the head of any red devil?"

Calhoun shook his head and stretched back out in his bedroll. He saw no reason to say good night to the two. He had seen a flash of accusation in O'Shea's eyes, and that was humorous to Calhoun. He got no joy out of it, but he figured it was a good thing that O'Shea would be on the defensive around him—and around Medicine Bear, too, for that matter.

CHAPTER

∗ 11 ∗

The morning broke cold and dismal, with thick clots of iron-gray clouds bunched in the sky. A heavy, cloying fog hung over the campsite, obscuring everything more than a few feet away. It was, all in all, a thoroughly unpleasant day. Calhoun thought it appropriate for this particular group.

Soon after, though, the sun cracked through the oppressive ceiling of clouds a little, spreading some weak light and fragile warmth. Calhoun came out of his little tent and stretched. Though the sun still seemed as if it were hiding behind a patch of canvas, he enjoyed its feeble heat.

"Hey, Calhoun," Whitcomb shouted. He was walking up the slope, having a hard time of it between the wet grass and the mud.

Calhoun turned and waited.

"When you aimin' to leave here?" Whitcomb asked, stopping in front of Calhoun. He was puffing.

Calhoun shrugged.

"I'm of a mind to stick here awhile." The soldier hesitated to say anything more.

"I figure you are," Calhoun said dryly. From hearing Whitcomb and O'Shea shouting to each other a few minutes ago, he knew that the two had lost some gear as the Platte River rose slightly over its banks. Just how much they lost remained to be seen.

Calhoun let Whitcomb squirm just a bit longer before he nodded. "Reckon we can wait till tomorrow."

Whitcomb nodded, his relief evident in his florid face. He turned and headed gingerly down the slope.

Calhoun turned a little and saw Medicine Bear standing outside his lodge, a blanket wrapped around his torso. "You heard?" he asked.

Medicine Bear nodded once, curtly, as if he was beyond such mundane things.

Calhoun shook his head in annoyance. Of course Medicine Bear wouldn't mind staying here awhile. He had a fine lodge, though somewhat smaller than he was used to. He was warm and dry. He had food and his woman to care for him as he wished. *Hell,* Calhoun thought, *I'd be happy to stay here indefinitely, too.*

He spit and rolled a cigarette. As he smoked it he wondered about his next move. He was hungry, certainly, and wanted hot coffee, too. Though the rain had stopped, however, everything was saturated, so it might be near to impossible to find fuel for a fire. The thought of another cold meal of jerky and water made his stomach growl in protest.

He flicked the cigarette butt away and squatted back in his shelter. He had no real choice. Reaching into the food bag, he pulled out some jerky. With a look of distaste, he started gnawing on it.

After his meal, such as it was, he began cleaning his weapons. He was, at times, almost fanatical about it. The guns—his pistols in particular—were his constant companions. They were what had kept him alive for almost thirty years. The revolvers, his wits, and a deep survival instinct. There wasn't much he could do to keep his wits or his instincts in good shape, so he took excellent care of his weapons.

He worked slowly, being in no great hurry. He had nothing else to do at the moment, and nowhere to go. As he worked he heard a soft rustling sound. Without lifting his head, he raised his eyes and peered. An inquisitive Fat Bear stood just outside his small shelter. He watched intently as Calhoun's swift, sure hands did their work.

Calhoun did not let on that he knew Fat Bear was there. He just continued working at his own pace.

Growing ever more curious, Fat Bear squatted and watched. Then he inched forward, losing some of his fear of this pale-skinned man. Still, after his brother's incident with the hairy-faced bluecoat, the child was not too sure about approaching these strange beings too closely.

Calhoun still did not acknowledge the boy. He was torn inside, ripped apart by the knowledge of what Fat Bear was, and of what his people had done to Lizbeth and Lottie. He could never forget that. Never! On the other hand, Fat Bear was just a child, a small, inquisitive, interested, normal boy. It didn't mean much in the great scheme of things that he was also a hated Sioux. No, he was just a boy.

Realizing that, though, did little to mollify Calhoun's anger. If the Sioux war party had never visited that

Kansas Territory farmstead, Lottie would be about this boy's age now, give or take a few moons. It was hard to hate such a small human, despite the dark skin, coal-black hair, and deep-set eyes.

"Want to see?" Calhoun suddenly said, looking up. He wasn't sure who was more surprised—himself or Fat Bear. With a smooth move, he half twirled the pistol so that its grip was facing the boy.

Fat Bear was so surprised that he had started, and then fell into the mud. His plump little bottom made a funny little splat. He looked shocked, then he giggled. The giggles grew, developing into a full-scale assault of laughter.

Calhoun smiled, shocking himself again. He could not remember the last time he had allowed himself an honest-to-goodness smile. This one was real, despite that it wasn't too big. A kernel of worry burrowed into his stomach, as if to say he would die soon and rot in hell for making the small, innocent expression.

He decided to not let it bother him. As soon as he decided that, he noted the smile and then it left. It had not been forced, but he would not let it linger either.

Fat Bear, on the other hand, was practically rolling with childish laughter. It was such an unusual noise in the otherwise tense camp that everyone else stopped to look for its source. Just past the edge of his small shelter, Calhoun could see Medicine Bear standing in regal splendor, looking with distaste and concern at his son. But he was too proud to say anything.

"I reckon your old man thinks you've been took by spirits or somethin'," Calhoun said softly.

Fat Bear finally got control of himself and sat crossed-legged in front of Calhoun. He was covered with mud but didn't seem to care. Calhoun had gone back to work on his Dragoon. The next thing he knew, Fat Bear was sticking his chubby little face inches from the gun. It was infinitely interesting to him.

"Aw, hell," Calhoun muttered under his breath. "Come here, boy," he said aloud, not quite believing what he was going to do. He set the pistol aside and grabbed the boy around the middle. Fat Bear's face revealed a little terror. "It's all right, boy," he said softly. He lifted the boy a little, turned him, and set him in his lap. Then he picked up the gun again.

With more gentleness than any watcher would have thought, Calhoun guided Fat Bear's hands through the process of cocking and dry-firing the big pistol. Through two shirts and two skins, Calhoun could feel Fat Bear's heart racing with the excitement of the moment.

The two stayed that way for a while, with Fat Bear growing more animated. Once Calhoun looked up and saw Medicine Bear staring balefully at him. He had no idea of what was going on in the warrior's head. He didn't care much either, other than to hope that Medicine Bear was a little irritated.

Another time he spotted Painted Sky staring at him and her son. Her face, too, was telling nothing about her feelings.

Finally, though, Calhoun had the itch to be doing

something else. "That's enough, boy," he said gruffly. "Go on to your ma now."

A suddenly solemn Fat Bear nodded and then ran to his lodge. Calhoun ignored the uneasy stare the two soldiers threw at him as he loaded the Dragoon and slid it into the holster. He spent another half hour or so with the other Dragoon. That done, he stepped outside.

The sun was stronger, and that combined with the humidity that lingered in the air gave the day a hot, leaden feel. Calhoun was just as glad they had decided to stay here—traveling in this kind of weather was not pleasant for either man or horse.

He saw to his animals and then just wandered a bit, working his feelings over in his mind. He was not usually given to such things, but this trip had, so far, been a full-out assault on his senses: the irritation at Whitcomb and O'Shea; his undying hatred for Medicine Bear, sublimated only because of his task; the desire to couple with Painted Sky; his newfound friendship, if that's what it could be called, with Fat Bear. The only one on the trip who had not affected him much one way or the other was the baby, Red Arrow.

Since he was unused to dealing with such things, he could come to no conclusion. Finally he shrugged and walked back to his "camp." He hung his bedroll over a bush to dry and then sorted through his supplies, separating out what was not needed.

As he prowled around in the increasing heat of the day, he kept his eye peeled for dry firewood. He just couldn't bear the thought of another meal of jerky, one minus coffee. He didn't find much, but he figured it was enough for a small fire. That would get him a pot of coffee and maybe even some roasted meat.

He dropped the firewood next to his tent and hauled his saddle over to where his hobbled horse was grazing. He saddled and bridled it and rode out, figuring that the others would appreciate fresh meat as much as he would.

Before long, he jumped a small herd of antelope. They bolted, racing off to the west. He dropped the rope to the pack mule. "Time to show your stuff, horse," he said quietly as he spurred the animal.

Calhoun knew the horse could not keep up with the antelope for very long, so he pulled one of the Walkers from the saddle holster. The big, heavy pistol had more stopping power than the Dragoon. He closed in on two antelope bounding almost together. Calhoun fired four times. Three shots hit, while the fourth winged off one of the antelope's horns.

Calhoun pulled up and shoved his pistol away. He turned the horse, patting the animal's lightly sweating neck. He rode back to the mule, which had pretty much stayed where he had left it, and grabbed the rope. A few minutes later both antelope were lashed down on the mule's back and Calhoun was heading toward camp.

He dropped one antelope outside Medicine Bear's lodge and the other at the soldiers' new camp, up the slope and some yards to the west of Calhoun's tent. "I'll be back for my portion directly," he said curtly. He rode off and took care of the mule and horse. He lugged his tack to his makeshift tent and dropped it just inside. That's when he noticed his small pile of firewood was gone.

Red flashed in Calhoun's eyes as he glared around. Painted Sky was butchering the antelope already, her back to Calhoun. Fat Bear played nearby. The boy suddenly stopped and waved at Calhoun, who nodded curtly. Fat Bear wandered over to Calhoun.

"Wrong?" he asked in his imperfect English.

It took a moment for Calhoun to figure out what Fat Bear was getting at. He nodded. He pointed. "Somebody took my wood," he said, realizing that the child probably could not understand him.

Fat Bear nodded solemnly. "Blue take," he said, still nodding.

"What?" Calhoun asked, trying to understand.

"Blue take." Fat Bear pointed to where Whitcomb and O'Shea had set their camp.

"Obliged, boy," Calhoun growled. He swung around and strode purposefully toward the soldiers. He grabbed O'Shea, whose back was to him, by the coat and dragged him around. "Where the hell's my firewood, boy?" he demanded.

"I don't know what you mean," O'Shea said unconvincingly.

"I'll ask one more time, boy," Calhoun said fiercely. "Then I'll gut you."

"There," O'Shea said, pointing. He was shaken and scared. "Sarge made me take it."

"Pick it up and carry it back, boy."

"But, Sarge'll—"

"Sarge ain't gonna do shit to you, boy. Now git." Calhoun gave O'Shea a shove.

As O'Shea started grabbing up firewood Calhoun moved off. He had heard Whitcomb whistling down toward the river. When Calhoun found the sergeant, he was sitting on a short, low shelf over the river. He had a string in the water and was still whistling.

The sound stopped abruptly as Calhoun walked up behind Whitcomb, knelt, and wrapped a strong right hand around his neck. "You mess with me or my stuff again, soldier boy, and there won't be enough of you left to feed a sparrow."

Whitcomb gurgled.

"You got somethin' to say?"

"Yes." It was garbled and strangled, but clear enough.

Calhoun relented only a little.

"I'll have your ass for this, Calhoun," the sergeant snarled. "I'll—"

Calhoun choked off the response again. "Just mind what I say, soldier boy." He let Whitcomb go, rose, turned, and walked off. O'Shea was just finishing with the last load of firewood. "Bring the antelope next, boy," he ordered.

Scared, O'Shea nodded. He hated Wade Calhoun as much as he had ever hated anyone. First the incident at Fort Laramie, where Calhoun had made a fool of him. Now this. And maybe it was Calhoun who had whacked him on the head when he was trying to have a good time with that Indian woman. That thought had crossed his mind more than once.

He still could not decide whether it was Calhoun or that red devil Medicine Bear.

Giving his anger free rein, O'Shea grabbed the antelope and jerked it up and over his shoulder. He did not care that blood splattered his uniform. It was so filthy with mud and such that it didn't matter. He carted the animal away and threw it down. As he turned, Calhoun hammered him across the bridge of the nose with a forearm.

O'Shea went down in a sprawl of arms and legs.

"Let that be a lesson to you, soldier boy," Calhoun said evenly. "Now get the hell away from me."

O'Shea scrambled away, more scared than angry right now.

CHAPTER * 12 *

Calhoun was glad to be on the move again. Even one day of hanging around with people he hated—and who reciprocated that feeling—was tedious to him. Besides, the longer they were on the trail, the sooner they would get to Fort Kearny and his odious service would be done.

As usual, Calhoun rode at the rear of the caravan. He was not fond of eating dust, as was the case in such a position, but it was far better than having two hate-filled soldiers riding behind him. Especially after last night.

Calhoun always slept like a cat. An inner sense seemed to be constantly on the alert, no matter how deeply he was sleeping. It let the normal night sounds pass by, but anything out of the ordinary, no matter how slight, woke him, instantly alert, and usually with a pistol in hand. Over the years he had come to a point that when he awoke in such cases, he did not move, other than slipping his hand onto a pistol, until he could find out what it was that had disturbed him. Such a skill was handy for staying alive in a harsh land, and usually disconcerted whoever or whatever was creeping around.

Calhoun had butchered the antelope and cooked a

fair-sized portion of it. He cut off a little—no more than a couple of pounds—and brought it to the soldiers. Stopping ten feet away, he tossed the bloody, raw meat. Whitcomb started and managed to catch it before it hit the ground. He stared blackly at Calhoun.

The rest of the antelope Calhoun put in a sack and hoisted up a tree to keep it out of the clutches of whatever predators might be lurking about. Finally he stretched out on his bedroll.

He didn't know how much later it was when he awoke, but some soft scuffling or scraping had woken him. He lay there a few moments, hand on a Dragoon, all his senses alert.

He heard something again, but still could not figure out what it was. He was fairly certain, though, that it did not bode well for him. He slid out of the bedroll, slithered out of the small tent, and moved in the general direction of Medicine Bear's lodge.

Finally he stopped and lay there, listening, waiting. Clouds had come back up in the late afternoon, but were breaking up again. The moon slid into one of the openings in the clouds, allowing Calhoun to see.

He spotted Whitcomb creeping toward the head of his bedroll and O'Shea inching toward the foot. The clouds closed over the gap, and Calhoun pushed himself up. He glided silently away from his tent, then curled back a few yards to his right. That brought him up behind Whitcomb, who was crawling with exaggerated slowness toward Calhoun's shelter.

Calhoun walked silently up behind Whitcomb and set his foot down hard on his back. He cocked a

Dragoon and aimed it at the back of the soldier's head. Whitcomb could not see the pistol, of course, but he was astute enough to know where it was pointed.

"Goin' somewhere, soldier boy?" Calhoun asked sarcastically. It was a pity, he thought. In general, he liked soldiers. He had worked with them often enough, and as a rule found them to be decent, honorable men. Of course, there were always a few idiots in any bunch. He figured that Whitcomb and O'Shea were quite qualified for such designation.

He got no answer from Whitcomb, but that did not bother him. "Best call off the other goddamn fool lest I get nervous."

Whitcomb had many faults in life, but being so stupid as to risk his life for nothing was not among them. "Front and center, Private," he called, voice muffled a little by the grass, as well as Calhoun's boot on his back.

"You all right, Sarge?" O'Shea said.

"Not exactly."

O'Shea, lying out there in the dark, wondered what was wrong. He thought for a minute of just hightailing it, but then he figured that someone would find him sooner or later. That was not a pleasant thought, considering that anyone who caught up to him would not feel too kindly disposed toward him.

O'Shea stood. With his Colt Dragoon cap-and-ball six-shooter in hand, he headed through the darkness toward . . . what he did not know.

"Toss the piece away, soldier boy."

Calhoun's low, rough voice coming out of the darkness startled O'Shea. So much so that he almost jerked his finger on the trigger. Sweating, he eased the Colt's hammer down and threw the weapon into the darkness.

"Walk forward."

O'Shea did as he was told, stopping only when he had stepped on Whitcomb's outstretched hand. He teetered on one foot for a moment, knowing that his next step would land his foot on Whitcomb's head. He managed to regain his balance and stepped back in one pace.

"We got a problem here, boys," Calhoun said. "And should we not fix it, somebody's gonna get killed. I don't plan for it to be me."

"What do you suggest?" Whitcomb asked. He was not only angry now, he was humiliated. He intended to make Calhoun pay.

Calhoun moved his foot. "Stand." When Whitcomb did so, he said, "We got us a job to do—gettin' that redskin devil to Fort Kearny."

"So?" Whitcomb asked, brushing grass and mud off the front of his clothes. Another break in the clouds came, and he got his first look at Calhoun. The sight did not improve his mood any. Calhoun looked like a veritable harbinger of death.

"I suggest we do that the best we can. Quick as we can, too. That done, we can settle our differences."

Whitcomb stared at him. He was not a trustful man in the best of circumstances, and he was not sure he could trust Calhoun to live up to his word. Were the situations reversed, he figured he'd get to

Fort Kearny, pick up his money, and then hightail it for the nearest saloon and brothel. He wouldn't wait around for two men to come gunning for him.

Wade Calhoun, however, was rather different from most men Whitcomb had encountered. He was hard as granite and utterly fearless. He could—and did—kill efficiently, ruthlessly, yet he derived no pleasure from it. Calhoun hated the Sioux, too. Whitcomb could see that in his eyes. He didn't know why Calhoun hated the Sioux so much, but it was plainly evident.

Whitcomb shook his head. "You got a deal." He considered it possible that he could lull Calhoun into a sense of security, then lash out when the man was least expecting it. And, the sergeant figured, if Calhoun stayed wary all the way to Fort Kearny, then he himself would just get some extra help from the soldiers there. Five or six troopers would have no trouble gunning down Calhoun.

Calhoun didn't believe Whitcomb for a moment. He knew the sergeant would come at him as soon as he thought he had the upper hand. *Let him think that,* Calhoun thought. *He'll pay dear for it.* "Fine," he said.

Whitcomb and O'Shea eased around and started off.

"Just one more thing, boys," Calhoun added. When the two soldiers turned back to face him, he said, "You come at me again and I'll kill you." There was no questioning the sincerity in his voice.

Despite the interruptions, Calhoun slept well and was up before anyone else except Painted Sky. As he stood just outside his little tent and stretched, Painted Sky was just coming up the slope from the river. She carried a small bucket of water. She nodded hello at him, without really looking at him. It was a trait of Indian women that Calhoun did not understand. They just never looked at a man full.

He nodded back, wondering about her. After she went into her lodge, Calhoun snorted in disgust with himself. However, he figured he now knew why he was drawn to the woman despite the fact that she was a Sioux. It had been several days since he had had a woman, and he hadn't had Naomi nearly enough to make up for the loneliness of all his time on the trail before reaching Fort Laramie. He felt better now, having puzzled that out.

He walked down to the river and washed himself up a little. The water was still running fast and cold, but it was shrinking already. He went back to his tent and rekindled the fire. With a couple big cups of coffee and a heaping portion of antelope in him, he was ready to be on the trail.

"Let's move," he shouted, startling some birds. They had been chirping and singing as the day broke, but they fell silent as Calhoun's harsh voice intruded on them.

"Go to hell," Whitcomb answered. He sounded mighty sleepy.

"You got ten minutes," Calhoun said. "Then I'll turn your animals loose."

"All right, goddammit," Whitcomb groused.

It was more like half an hour, but Calhoun wasn't really in all that much of a hurry. He simply wanted to get the others moving. He was packed—all except his tin mug, which was filled with the last of the pot's coffee—and watching Painted Sky take down her lodge. It never ceased to amaze him. She could put the thing up by herself in twenty minutes or so. It came down in three or four.

Finally he kicked some mud and dirt over his little fire and hauled himself onto the splotchy horse. They left, riding mostly in a single file, following the rough, ragged course of the Platte on the south side. Across the river, to the north, there were sand hills, and along the banks were stunted cedar trees and thorny brush. To the south were dull, rolling plains, the summer grass burned down low by the heat of the sun.

It was early afternoon when Calhoun noticed the slow-moving puff of dust to the southeast. It was moving toward his group. He kept an eye on the cloud as he rode. Out here, it could be Pawnees again, maybe Osages or Kickapoos or Pota-wotamies. It could even be Sioux or Arikaras heading home from the war trail. It was possibly a group of white men, but there wasn't much reason out here for white civilians to be roaming.

Calhoun looked at his companions. Whitcomb and O'Shea seemed oblivious. Medicine Bear saw the coming cloud, of that Calhoun was sure, though the Sioux had given no indication whatsoever that he saw anything out of the ordinary.

It kept coming, inexorably, until even the two soldiers were aware of it. Whitcomb raised his right hand as he came to a stop. Everyone else stopped, too. "Calhoun, front and center," the sergeant hollered without looking back. He figured this was a good time to humiliate the man who had humiliated him.

A few moments later he realized that he heard nothing behind him but horses snuffling and shaking their manes. He risked a quick look over his shoulder. Calhoun still sat on his horse, leaning a little forward, resting his forearms on the wide saddle horn.

"Dammit," Whitcomb swore under his breath. He had been made to look the fool again. He half stood and turned in the stirrups. "I'd be obliged for you to come up here, Mr. Calhoun," he said sarcastically.

"I'm comfortable," Calhoun said evenly.

Whitcomb flushed with anger. His rage was fanned by the small smile on Medicine Bear's face. *The insolent Sioux son of a bitch,* he thought. *I'll kill him, too, once I'm done with that goddamn Calhoun.*

He looked to the front again. The cloud was still coming. Though it was some ways off yet, he could see it was a group of riders. To his left, a couple hundred yards off, were some brush and a few stunted cedar trees. It wasn't the best cover, but it was all they had right now. He waved his hand in the air and rode off again, hoping that the others were following.

It was with some relief that he learned they did. He reached the thicket, stopped, and turned his horse in a quarter circle. The others were moving into the brush already. No one said anything.

Calhoun stopped next to Whitcomb. "They're whites," he said.

"How the hell do you know that?" Whitcomb asked, frustrated.

"The way they ride," Calhoun said evenly.

Whitcomb was uncertain. Calhoun had a reputation as a top scout. Or at least he used to. Still, Whitcomb felt more than a little that Calhoun was putting him on again somehow, trying to make him look like a fool yet again.

"Why don't you go on out there and greet them, then?" Whitcomb asked, some of his nervousness and anger coming out with the words.

"Didn't say they was good white men. Just that they're white, and not Injins."

"Bastard," Whitcomb muttered, glaring at Calhoun. "Why the hell did the major ever give you this job?"

"Needed someone he could trust to get old redskin there to Fort Kearny."

"What the hell's that mean?" Whitcomb asked huffily.

Calhoun shrugged.

"Goddamn you, Calhoun, you son of a bitch, I'm about—"

Calhoun pointed. "They're comin'."

Whitcomb angrily jerked his head around. "Shit," he breathed. As much as he hated to admit it, Calhoun had been right—they were white men riding at a good clip toward them, and were within a hundred yards or so. He straightened his rumpled uniform blouse as best he could and waited.

Within minutes ten men were pulling to a stop

maybe thirty feet away from Calhoun and Whitcomb.

A hard-eyed man coated with trail dust and sweat
moved ahead a few feet. He was a tall, rangy fellow,
with a square jaw and weather-wrinkled features.
Several days' worth of stubble covered his face, and
he had a short, clipped mustache. A wad of chaw
puffed out one cheek.

"What're you boys doin' out here?" the man
asked roughly.

"I might ask the same of you, mister," Calhoun
said, voice as hard-edged as the other's.

The man shrugged. "None of your goddamn business." He paused and leaned over some to spit some
tobacco juice. "We ain't time for fartin' around with
assholes like you. Now, what're you doin' out here?"

CHAPTER
* 13 *

Calhoun had rolled a cigarette and fired it up. He spit a loose bit of tobacco out and turned cold, hard eyes on the man. "Unless you want to lose a couple of your men, pal, best tell 'em to keep their hands away from their weapons," he said coolly.

"She-it," the man scoffed.

"I'm glad you boys come along," Whitcomb said with relief. He figured now he could get out from under Calhoun's pressure.

"Eat shit, bluebelly." He paused and spit again. "Now, I ain't gonna ast you but this one mo' time, boys—what's your business out heah." His drawl was thicker than Calhoun's.

"We're takin' some goddamn Sioux buck and his bitch wife to Fort Kearny for some goddamn pow-wow or somethin'," Whitcomb said. He was no longer sure he had found allies here.

The man came alert at the mention of the Indians. "A Sioux you say, boy?" His voice was cold and hard as a bucket of nails in the winter.

"Yep," Whitcomb said eagerly. Here was someone who knew about such things. A man who wasn't scared off by the presence of one goddamn Indian.

"Hand the bastard over."

"No," Calhoun said flatly. His right hand rested on the grip of a Dragoon. He knew he could not get them all, but his death would not come cheaply. He would make sure of that.

"Look, peckerwood, I ain't got time for shittin' around with the likes of you or that chickenshit bluebelly. Now do as I say and ain't nobody gonner get hurt."

"The army'll have our asses for that," Whitcomb said. He thought the idea of handing Medicine Bear over to these men was fine, but he didn't want to come off sounding too eager.

"And we'll have yo' asses you don't."

"Now, just wait a minute, here, mister," Whitcomb said, trying to reason with the man.

"Name's Cal Bohannon. From Osage Creek in Kansas Territory."

"Sergeant Gerard Whitcomb. First Mounted Infantry, Fort Laramie."

"Big goddamn deal," Bohannon said. "Now give us over that buck. Might's well toss in the bitch, too."

"What're we supposed to do with the brats?" Whitcomb asked. As soon as he said it, he knew he had been a fool.

Bohannon's eyes lit up. "Sioux brats?"

"Two of 'em," Whitcomb said with a sick feeling in his stomach. It wasn't that he all of a sudden decided he liked Indian kids; it was just that he realized too late that he could've used the children as a bargaining chip somehow. Once he opened his mouth, there was no going back, though.

"Bring 'em out."

"I don't think—"

"I know you don't, bluebelly. Now, I ain't of a mind to set here and jaw with you peckerwoods all goddamn day. We got business to see to, and it's business best done sooner than late."

"What's your interest in this, Bohannon?" Calhoun asked.

"None of your goddamn business."

Calhoun casually flipped his cigarette away. It landed near Bohannon's horse, though not close enough to bother the animal. Bohannon had seen it, though. "Might make us more disposed to hand them Injins over was you to say why you wanted 'em."

"Reasonable enough," Bohannon said with a nod. He pulled off his hat and wiped a dirty sleeve across his sweaty forehead. "Damn, it's hot," he said to no one in particular. He put the hat back on. "Bunch of goddamn Sioux come ridin' through our area a couple days ago." His eyes flicked from Whitcomb to Calhoun. He thought he saw some recognition in Calhoun's eyes.

"Bastards burned down a couple homesteads and butchered a passel of good, God-fearin' folk, from younkers right up to a couple grannies. Righteous people they was all of 'em." Rage sat inside his chest. "Best we can figger, the bucks carted off a couple women and a few little'uns. We aim to get 'em back."

Calhoun's hand tightened on the pistol grip. A blinding fury flared up out of his heart, roared up his throat, and caught fire in his brain. He found it hard to breathe, and though he could see everything before him, it was all tinged by a hot red film.

"You all right, there, hoss?" Bohannon asked. He wasn't really all that interested, but Calhoun seemed like he had seen a ghost.

"Yes," Calhoun said in a strangled voice.

"Good," Bohannon said. "Now, hand over them savages."

"No," Calhoun said, voice still ragged. He wanted more than anything to turn around and kill Medicine Bear, Painted Sky, and the two children right here and now. But he could not bring himself to do that. He couldn't even give them over to Bohannon's men. He had made a promise, and he would keep it, no matter how personally difficult it was.

There was also the matter of his conscience. He could not kill Painted Sky, or Fat Bear and Red Arrow. That would place him on a level with the savages who had butchered his family. He refused to do that. One-on-one with Medicine Bear, that was another story. He looked forward to that—after getting to Fort Kearny.

"What the hell you mean no, boy?" Bohannon demanded.

"Just what I said." Some of the fury was filtering out of him, enough so that his voice and demeanor had returned to something approaching normal.

"Goddammit," Bohannon said in exasperation, "there's a half-dozen good folk layin' butchered back there. And some young'uns in the hands of those bastards. If you only knew how—"

"I do know," Calhoun said, fighting the renewed wave of rage. "Goddammit, I do. . . ." His voice trailed off, but his face was etched in sharp angles like flint.

Bohannon squinted at him. "Then what's your problem, boy?"

"You," Calhoun said, gaining control over himself.

"Me?" Bohannon was surprised.

"Yep. You're a pain in my ass."

Bohannon started, and his craggy face bunched up in furrows. "I ain't so sure I appreciate such a thing," he said, befuddled as well as angry.

Calhoun shrugged. "Don't mean shit to me what you—"

Someone slammed Calhoun on the back of the head, and he crumpled off his horse. Things got fuzzy for him then. He was aware of much suddenly going on, but it all was covered with a film and seemed to be happening at a far slower pace than was normal.

A dim, faraway-sounding screech erupted, and then a buckskin-clad demon burst forth from the brush. Arrows flew from his bow. Suddenly all the men behind Bohannon ripped out their guns. They charged forward, firing pistols.

Medicine Bear went down, body riddled with bullets, but not before he had taken out three of the men. As Medicine Bear fell his war cry changed to a death chant. He tried to stand, ready to kill more, but he was having trouble. One leg was broken in three places, and blood poured from a dozen wounds. He got to his feet, his singing weak. Another shot and he was down for good.

Calhoun was groggy right from the start, and he fought hard to keep the blackness from overwhelming him. As Medicine Bear burst from the brush he struggled to reach the screen of brambles a few yards away. He was vaguely aware of the Sioux warrior being slammed to the ground by gunfire. Still he struggled on.

He stopped, coated with sweat, for a breather. He slowly craned his head around, weakly.

Painted Sky shot out from the brush and turned hard right, whipping her horse hard. She was fifty yards away before one of Bohannon's men dropped to one knee and fired at her with his rifle. She fell from the horse.

As Calhoun scrunched along, heading through the thickets toward the river, he heard shouts and scared crying. Fat Bear's angry little voice drifted over the land.

"Grab them goddamn kids," someone yelled.

"Where's that saddle bum?" another roared.

"In the thicket," O'Shea said. Calhoun recognized the voice, despite the excitement in it.

"Let's go finish him off," Whitcomb said. His hatred for Calhoun overflowed.

"No!" O'Shea shouted.

"No?" Whitcomb said, voice sharp. "What the hell do you mean no, boy? I give you an order, I expect it to be obeyed straight off."

"He's hurt bad, Sarge."

"So? You gettin' soft all of a sudden?"

"Nope. Let me finish what I was gonna say."

"Get on with it, then."

"He's hurt bad, like I said, and I don't think he can get far. Let's just leave him. We leave him and he'll die of thirst or starvation. Maybe the wolves'll get him. And if any goddamn Injuns come along, they'll be sure to make short work of him."

Whitcomb laughed harshly. "Damn, I like that idea."

Bohannon told one of his men, Bo Gardner, to check on the others that were down. "It don't look good for 'em," he added, then turned to look at O'Shea, who had Fat Bear and Red Arrow in his grasp. "Gimme them little bastards."

O'Shea shook his head. The children were nothing to him, but he wanted to use them for his own purposes. "I'll be glad to give 'em to you boys, if you let me"—he paused—"and Sergeant Whitcomb ride along with you." He was not fond of Whitcomb, but figured there would be less trouble if he included the noncom in the deal.

"No skin off my ass," Bohannon said. He had no liking for the two soldiers, but since it looked like he had just lost three of his men, two experienced guns would be a good idea. Besides, one never knew when it might be handy to have a couple of soldiers around, especially if they could be gotten rid of in a hurry, should that seem necessary.

O'Shea nodded, then asked, "What're you gonna do with them kids?"

"You worried about 'em?" Bohannon made it sound like a curse.

"Nope. Just curious."

Bohannon nodded. "Plan to use 'em to trade for

some of our friends who've been took. Or as bait for a trap, if the first don't work."

O'Shea nodded. It sounded fair enough to him.

Bo Gardner came back. "Lije, Lonnie, and Mitch have passed on to the great beyond."

"Damn that son-of-a-bitchin' savage bastard," Bohannon growled. He was close to all three men who had died. Mitch Cleland was his brother-in-law; Lonnie Cofield a distant cousin; and Lije Bates was a longtime friend. "All right, Bo, you and the others get them three on their horses. We ain't got time to bury 'em now. We'll do it soon's we can."

"What're you gonna be up to, Cal?" Gardner asked.

"I got me some whittlin' to do."

Gardner nodded while Whitcomb and O'Shea stood there wondering just what Bohannon meant. They learned soon enough, and the sight of Bohannon carving parts out of Medicine Bear's corpse was sickening.

Calhoun had missed most of the conversation, because of the grayness that still swarmed around him and the distance he had put between them and himself. He wondered about the children and figured they were in dire straits, but there was little he could do about anything now.

He crawled toward the river and plopped his face in, hoping the cold, swift water would help revive him. He got his head out of the river just before unconsciousness overtook him.

✴   ✴   ✴

Calhoun came to slowly, fighting the mist of unconsciousness. He lay there a while, partly lulled by the rushing of the water so near to him. Something else was around, too, but he couldn't quite figure out what. He cracked open his eyes, grateful for the twilight dimness and the cover of brush. He wasn't sure who was more startled, himself or the coyote that had been sniffing around him.

"Git, you little bastard," he growled. The short phrase made his head rattle, clack, and throb. The coyote skittered away and stood looking balefully at him. Calhoun ignored it.

Finally, though, he knew he had to get up. The effort to do so left him reeling, the pain in his head so bad he wanted to vomit. He would've given in to the feeling if he thought it would have helped him any.

"Jesus," he muttered, clenching his teeth against the smashing throb in his head and the back of his neck. Over the years he had suffered several bullet wounds that were less painful than this. He sat for what seemed like a long time before summoning up the strength and desire to try to stand.

He made it, though, eventually, but he had to lean against a small tree to stay on his feet. Gingerly he reached around and felt the back of his head. There was a good-sized knot just above where the neck and head met. He felt matted blood there, too.

Calhoun gritted his teeth and let his eyes go out of focus. Then he drew in long, deep breaths. He released them slowly. Each cycle of breathing like that helped to settle him an infinitesimal amount.

After what he judged to be about ten minutes, he stopped and let his eyes focus again. His head still throbbed and pulsed as if it had a life of its own, but his knees no longer felt quite so wobbly, and he no longer had the urge to puke.

He shoved away from the tree and staggered toward where the short, furious battle had taken place. There was blood in dozens of places, and the ground was trampled. He found his hat, looking little more battered than it usually was. He put it on.

Calhoun squared his shoulders, knowing he had to go check on Medicine Bear. He knew instinctively that the Sioux had been butchered. He had seen the handiwork of Indians before, just as he had seen that performed by whites. It was never pretty and this was no exception. Medicine Bear had been savagely mauled by someone who was both experienced and enraged. What had been left had been worked over by scavengers. Calhoun figured the coyote was one of them.

Calhoun could spare no sympathy for the Indian. Left up to him, he would've done the same thing to Medicine Bear.

CHAPTER

✳ 14 ✳

Calhoun walked a few yards way from Medicine Bear's mutilated corpse and sat on a rock to take stock of his situation. He had his two Dragoons and the backup Walker. He still had his bowie knife and the dirk in his boot. He had a little more ammunition in the belt pouch in the form of paper cartridges and two fully loaded cylinders.

He was afoot, though, since Bohannon had taken his horse—with his saddle. He had no food, no utensils, no bedroll. Well, he figured, he had been in worse spots before. He would make do.

The coyote was still hanging around, pacing back and forth ten yards or so away from Calhoun. Worse, it had been joined by several others. Calhoun figured they had been dining on Medicine Bear's body and had shuffled off out of the way when Calhoun had lurched up.

"Best get, you sons of bitches, or you'll be my supper tonight." He picked up a small stone and threw it at one coyote. It hit the animal, but with little force. Still, the canine looked surprised to Calhoun. He picked up another small stone and threw it.

The coyote finally seemed to understand that this was one meal that was just not going to roll over and get eaten. The animal loped off, looking for more cooperative prey. His companions followed.

Calhoun stood again. It was a little easier this time. He lurched off, checking out the rest of the area. He found some blood by the river a short way and figured that Painted Sky had been shot. Evidently not badly, though, he thought, since there was no body around and little evidence that she had gone off by herself. He figured that one of the men in the posse had winged her and then took her along. She would be having a hard time of it, Calhoun knew.

He thought he remembered the men talking about the two children. It seemed as if they were going to keep them alive, at least for now, and use them in some way. It would make sense, in some ways. They could trade the youngsters for some of the white captives.

He sighed and turned back to where he had been sitting. He prowled through the brush along the way, looking for signs. There was not much to be seen that he didn't already know. About the only thing he didn't know was who had hit him. By the placement of the men, he assumed it had been Private Ian O'Shea. Calhoun figured that was just one more score to settle.

In order to do that, he would have to regain his health and then find someplace where he could get supplies and a horse. That meant he needed to get to a town, precious few of which were to be found in this barren country.

First, though, there was the matter of finding some food. He half regretted having chased the coyotes away. He had never eaten such flesh, but hell, it could be a lot worse. Anyway, the critters were gone, and now he would have to think of something else.

He started shuffling downriver. It was late in the day, and he felt like staying right where he had been. He figured, though, that Medicine Bear's body would be attracting even more scavengers, which he was in no mood or shape to deal with. Besides, the place reeked of man scent, and that would keep most all of the game animals away. If he could get a little distance between himself and the blood, he might have a decent chance of finding some game.

He could not walk for long now, though, not when it felt like a railroad spike was being driven into his skull with each step. He judged he had come half a mile or so and figured that was enough. He was sweating and shaky.

"Jesus," he muttered as he eased himself down on a log. In a few minutes he felt a little better. Afternoon was fading fast, though, and he needed some food. He lurched down to the river and dunked his head in. It revived him some. Drinking helped a little more.

He sat again and checked his two Dragoons. A few of the caps had fallen off, and he replaced them. In normal circumstances, he would have emptied, cleaned, and reloaded the revolvers, but he did not have his cleaning materials. Worse, he had precious little extra powder and ball. He would have to leave the revolvers the way they were. He didn't think he had gotten close enough to the water to get his powder wet. And if he had, there was a good chance the extra ammunition in his pouch had suffered the same fate. He would have to trust to luck, which for him usually was in pretty short supply.

He quickly gathered up a small pile of firewood. If he did manage to shoot something, he would be able to cook it. Just before the blackness of the night descended, he spotted a raccoon waddling down toward the water. He eased out a pistol and cocked it as silently as he could.

The raccoon heard it and froze for a moment to try to determine where the danger lay. It was his undoing. Soon after, a gutted, skinned raccoon was roasting over a small, aromatic fire. Calhoun rolled a smoke while he waited. When the cigarette was done, he figured it was time to eat. He didn't have the patience now to wait until the meat was fully cooked. He gobbled down bits of the gamy meat, thinking how well it would have gone with some hot coffee.

He settled for several long drafts of river water. He felt almost human again, though his head was still paining him more than a little. Stretching out near the fire, he pulled his hat down over his face, and using his arms as a pillow, he let sleep take him.

He felt considerably better the next morning. The knot at the back of his skull had shrunk a little and his head no longer pounded. It was instead just a dull, persistent ache. With a slightly better outlook, Calhoun finished off the raccoon meat. Then he set off, leaving the wide, muddy Platte River and heading southwest. He hoped to meet up with the

Medicine River. He made better time than he thought he would, but nowhere near as good as usual.

He began running low on energy shortly after noon, and his pace slackened considerably. The ache in his head, which had returned, and the fierce sun slamming down on him conspired to slow him down. He did not make the Medicine that day, and so he spent a night on the empty prairie. The only thing that went right for him was being able to shoot a small deer. With a buffalo-chip fire, he was well fed, if thirsty.

His thirst was beginning to worry him. He had no way to carry water, and so would have to rely on streams and rivers. If he didn't reach the Medicine the next day, he knew he would be in real trouble.

He slept wearily, dreaming at one point that a herd of buffalo was stampeding over him. That woke him and he sat up, sweating and with pistol in hand. When he realized it had only been a dream, he cursed, put his revolver away, and went back to sleep.

He hit the Medicine at midmorning. He was moving pretty slowly by then, weariness weighing him down. His tongue felt swollen from thirst and his mouth was sticky. When he finally spotted the river, he was certain he was hallucinating. Not until he was standing knee-deep in the water did he realize it was real.

He walked back to the bank. Worried a little, he unhooked his gun belt and put it aside. He also pulled his cigarette fixings and matches from his shirt pocket and tossed them on the holstered guns. He even pulled out his backup pistol and set it with the rest of his gear. He hated being without any of his revolvers, even for a little, but right now he could not afford to have the powder get wet.

Feeling much lighter, he went back to the river and sat down in it, letting the cool water rush over him. He dunked his head in and drank deeply. Water had never tasted quite so good to him. In a few minutes, sated, he strolled out of the water. On the rocky, muddy bank, he lay down, letting the wind and the sun dry him.

A couple of hours later he headed off again, following the river. He wanted to stay put a day or so, to see if he could regain some of his strength, but he wanted some cover. He walked until he found a place about three miles on where several cottonwoods spread their leafy shade over tangled brush, fallen trees, and heavy undergrowth.

Just as he made his way into the thorny brush, a startled deer jumped a few feet away. The animal bounded off to Calhoun's left. He jerked out his Dragoon and fired. He was quite annoyed with himself when it took two shots to down the deer.

He stayed there the rest of that day and all the next. He ate venison every hour or so, it seemed, and frequently sprawled prone at the side of the river and drank. To keep himself occupied, he smoked some of the deer meat so he would be able to carry it with him.

He also wondered about what drove him. He had wanted to die ever since Lizbeth and Lottie had been killed. Indeed, to some it seemed as if Wade Calhoun was on a collision course with death. But his survival instincts had kept him going. Yesterday, for example, it would have been so easy to just give up and lie down, letting life fade.

He couldn't do that, though, sometimes to his regret. This time, at least, he had something of a reason. He vowed he would find the men who had left him to die. They would pay the price. He wanted his horse back, too, and particularly his saddle.

To his surprise, he thought about the two Sioux children. They deserved better than to be left in the grasp of men like Cal Bohannon. He would try to get them back. What he would do with them then, he would decide when he had to.

Provisioned, more or less, he headed off the next morning. He was not quite sure where he was going. In places like this, he knew from experience, towns could spring up almost overnight. They could die just as quickly, too. He figured he would just tromp along until he saw some signs of habitation. They would be easy to spot: smoke from many chimneys would mingle in the blue sky; vultures and buzzards would circle endlessly, searching for some tossed-out morsel. If a settlement had been built back from the river a little ways, there would be wagon tracks to and from the river.

It was three more days before he found a well-used track heading mostly east from a flat spot on the riverbank. During his long trek he had soured, becoming bitter at having been so easily taken out. Anger at the men who had left him in such a sorry state drove him.

Still, he was in the poorest of humors when he finally wandered into a town. A painted, fairly well-maintained sign let visitors know they were entering Pawnee Flats.

Calhoun found the town typical of such places. Neat clapboard houses and businesses were mingled with tents and a few brick places. A haphazard grid of streets and alleys had been laid out. Wagons plied up and down what passed for a main street, which was fronted with businesses. There were plenty of saloons, which gave Calhoun some minor degree of cheer. Some of these towns out here frowned on saloons and the brothels that went with them.

Despite his foul mood, Calhoun took note of the women in two brick places. They were hard to miss, hanging out of their windows as they were, most dressed in nothing but a camisole—or less. They called out to him with a frankness not to be found in too many places. He almost smiled, and he waved back at a few of the women.

First, though, he wanted a couple of drinks. Then a decent meal. After that it would be time for paying the ladies a visit. That would just about wipe him out. He had less than thirty dollars on him, and it wouldn't go far.

He found a saloon that looked better than some dives he had been in, but was not too fancy. A sign over the entrance boldly proclaimed it to be Oldman's Saloon. He entered and headed to the bar. No one paid him too much attention. He ordered a shot and a beer. When the bartender had served them up,

Calhoun asked, "There a decent place to get some grub?"

"Marberry's. Three buildings up on this side."

Calhoun nodded. He downed the shot in one gulp and then took a sip of the beer. "Damn, that's good."

"We only serve the best."

Calhoun nodded. "Well, seems I've found a place to drink and one to eat. How about the other?"

The bartender smiled knowingly. "Little Maggie's. Brick place next door."

Calhoun nodded and indicated he wanted another shot. When the bartender had poured it, he asked, "*Little* Maggie?"

"Maggie's maybe five foot tall in her shoes. Weighs in at maybe ninety pounds." He chuckled. "She's a real goddamn hellion, that one."

Calhoun nodded.

"What're you doing here in Pawnee Flats?" the bartender asked. "If you don't mind my pryin'."

Calhoun shrugged. "I was headin' to Saint Joe from Fort Laramie when my goddamn horse stepped in a chuck hole. Pitched me clean off."

The bartender nodded. It was a hard thing to lose your horse that way. "You see any Injuns out there?"

"Nope." Calhoun poured the second shot down his pipes. "You been havin' trouble hereabout?"

"Some. Bunch of goddamn Sioux hit some farms and such over to Osage Creek. That's about twenty miles southwest of here."

"They do much damage?" Calhoun asked evenly.

"Killed six or seven folk, the way I hear it. Carried

off some kids and a couple women, too." The bartender refilled Calhoun's shot glass.

Calhoun tried to look sympathetic. "Anybody go after 'em?"

"Feller named Cal Bohannon formed himself a ranger company when it happened. Him and nine others. Bohannon was the cap'n, of course. They lit out after them red devils a couple weeks ago."

"Here's luck to 'em," Calhoun said, toasting with his glass. Then the whiskey slid smoothly down into his stomach. The bartender didn't even charge him for that one.

CHAPTER
✳ 15 ✳

Calhoun finished his beer, had another shot, then bid farewell to the bartender. He strolled to Marberry's Chop House and filled himself good on buffalo steak, potatoes, tasty fresh bread with gobs of thick butter, coffee, and a heaping portion of peach cobbler to top it off.

Sated, he leaned back in his chair, belched happily, and then rolled a smoke. He puffed as he sipped the last of his coffee.

Finally he pushed himself up, feeling a little sluggish from the meal, but happy, or as happy as he ever felt. He looked over the town as he wandered toward Little Maggie's. He surveyed some of the women who were hanging out the windows and brazenly making lewd suggestions to any man who passed.

Calhoun walked up the few steps and pushed open the front door. He faced a long hallway with doors to several rooms opening on both sides. A middle-aged black woman met him at the door and led him to one room. A small, smiling woman with garish makeup and several layers of cheap perfume walked elegantly toward him. She was not yet thirty, Calhoun guessed, and quite attractive. She wore an expensive silk dress, and the way she jiggled when she walked suggested she had no stays in her corset, if she even wore a corset.

She stuck out her tiny hand. "I'm Maggie," she said in a voice rich with the drawl of the bayou. She wrinkled up her nose. "Lord, you are a rank-smellin' feller, ain't you, friend?"

"Reckon I am," Calhoun admitted.

Maggie looked at the rugged, hard face and the steady brown eyes, and was forced to suppress a shudder. This man was a killer, that much she knew. Whether he was a generally peaceable man was another story. Still, he didn't seem crazy, just hard as a gun barrel.

"My girls don't favor such men, Mister . . . ?" Maggie said boldly.

"Wade Calhoun. You got some suggestions on how we can change their minds?"

"Take you a bath for an extra fifty cents."

"Alone?" His face hadn't changed, but for some reason Maggie suspected there was a smile buried under the grim exterior.

"Lord, no," she said with a saucy laugh. Calhoun's lips moved a tad, and Maggie thought that he was trying to smile. She felt a little sorry for a man who couldn't smile.

Calhoun nodded acceptance. "I'd be obliged was you to have someone get me some new duds while I'm occupied," he said.

"We can do that, Mr. Calhoun." She paused and smiled. She was interested in him, despite herself, for a couple of reasons. For one, he wasn't all that

bad-looking a fellow, plus she had always liked hard
men, ones with rough edges. Calhoun certainly fit
the bill on these counts. In addition, she saw him as
something of a challenge. Getting him to smile, or
better yet, to laugh, would take some doing. But she
was out of the performance part of her business
these days. She had taken on such challenges a
number of times in the past, and rarely failed. Now,
though, she left such things to the younger girls.

"Come," she said, taking one of his big, callused
hands in one of her dainty ones. "We'll go meet the
girls. I'd suggest Penelope. She's a bright, agile
thing, with hair the color of sunset. But the choice is
yours."

"I made my choice," he said softly.

Maggie stopped short and looked up at him. He
gazed levelly back. "No, Mr. Calhoun. That's out of
the question. I'm flattered that you'd say such a
thing, but . . . Well, I don't do that anymore."

"That's a lonely life, ma'am," Calhoun said, still
quietly. He had known Maggie had been sizing him
up, and he had seen the interest in her eyes. He was
arrogant enough to figure he could gentle her some.

Maggie's pale violet eyes darkened with anger,
but then lit up brightly. "I suppose it is, Mr. Calhoun.
But, alas, it is something I've chosen for myself."

"Damn fool thing," Calhoun responded bluntly.

"That might be, Mr. Calhoun. But it's what I've
chosen, and I plan to abide by that decision."

"A pity," Calhoun said with a sigh. "Well, then, I'll
say good-bye to you."

"What?" Maggie said, surprised. "Why?" She had

felt the fires beginning down in her loins, and she almost shuddered with the unexpected force of it.

"Lookin' at this fancy place, I suppose I ain't got enough cash."

Maggie froze, the fire inside dwindling quickly. *The son of a bitch,* she thought. *He's trying to get it free.*

"I ain't got but twenty-nine bucks and change," he said. He was almost always broke, and the admitting of it had lost any sense of shame to him long ago.

Maggie relaxed. It was enough for a session, and a long one at that.

"Besides, I ain't wanted here, I'll find someplace I am." Having established that she was interested, he now wanted to see just how interested she was.

Maggie was still looking at him, and still holding his hand. He had made no move for the door. Suddenly she made her decision. He might be playing her for a fool, but that was a chance she was willing to take. "Well, we can't have that now, can we?" she said in a husky whisper.

Calhoun shook his head.

Maggie searched his face and eyes. He showed no signs of gloating or of having pulled some trick. She began to feel she had made the right decision.

"Mazie!" Maggie yelled, breaking her gaze from Calhoun's and taking her hand back. She was suddenly all business.

A tall, heavyset black woman waddled in. "Yes'm?" She seemed worn-out, as if life had become a burden to her.

"Have one of the boys go to Hennessey's and get

Mr. Calhoun here a new pair of pants and a shirt."
She paused for a moment, looking Calhoun over.
"Best get him some longhandles and socks, too."

"Yes'm. Anythin' else?"

"First, get the boys who ain't busy to bring a tub
up to my room. The big tub, not that little one. I
went plenty of hot water for it. And bring soap."

"Yes'm." Mazie tottered off.

Maggie took Calhoun's hand again and led him up
the stairs. She opened a door and stepped through.
Calhoun remained impassive looking when he
entered the room, though he was impressed. It was
richly appointed, with fine furnishings, including the
large four-poster bed. Thick rugs were strewn about
the floor, and the room had at least six lanterns that
Calhoun could count. He had been in such opulence
only once or twice. It did not humble him, though it
did impress him.

He took a seat in a plush chair and waited. Maggie
was a little edgy, wondering if she had made the
right decision. So she paced.

The wait was only of several minutes' length.
Then there was a knock on the door. When Maggie
said, "Enter," three black men in their late teens
appeared. Two carried a long, narrow tin tub. The
other had two pails of steaming water in his hands.

It was all done efficiently. The tub was set down,
water poured in, and the young men were suddenly
gone. They returned moments later, each carrying
buckets of water. Several trips were made before
Maggie judged the tub full enough. Mazie then
brought a bar of soap and some fluffy toweling,

which she placed beside the tub. To Calhoun she handed a paper-wrapped package. "Yo' clothes, massah," she said dully.

"Thank you, Mazie."

She looked at him, startled, then covered up her confusion. There weren't too many men who would be polite to her and her kind. It always was a surprise on those rare occasions when it happened.

Finally Calhoun and Maggie were alone in the room. "Best get in before the water cools, Mr. Calhoun," she said, still businesslike.

Calhoun shrugged. He removed his gun belt and sheath and set them next to the tub, under some toweling. Then he quickly shed his clothes, unembarrassed, and got into the tub.

"Ain't you gonna help?" he asked as he began to lather himself up.

Maggie looked at him, startled. "I'd mess my face," she said, smiling wearily. She brushed her fingers along a cheek as she sat on the edge of the bed. She had had the bed made especially for her, and it was low to the floor so her feet would touch when she sat on the edge. It was one of the few ways in which she had fought to accommodate for her diminutive size.

She looked almost sad, Calhoun thought. "You'd look a heap better without all that paint, smell better without the perfume."

Maggie was startled again. She wondered about that. She hadn't really been shook up by a man since she started in this business, and that went back a few years. She wasn't old and thought she was still attractive. She wore the makeup more because the men expected it than because she liked it or because she thought it improved her looks. As for the perfume, she wore a lot more than she was comfortable breathing around, but she needed it as a defense against the stench of men like Calhoun; men who came off the trail stinking of blood and sweat, urine and dung.

"Kind of you to say so," she said, her smile a bit more real this time.

"It's true, I'd wager."

Suddenly Maggie laughed, the sound full, rich, and deeper than would be expected from such a small woman. "Maybe one day, Mr. Calhoun." She stood, though, and walked to the tub, where she knelt. She gingerly dipped her hands in the water and felt around a little, grinning when her hand encountered him and lingering a moment before moving on. She found the soap.

As she leaned forward to lather up his chest, Calhoun suddenly half turned and clamped his hands on her tiny waist. He hoisted her up, seemingly without effort, turned back, and plopped her in the water.

Maggie screeched. Soaking wet almost to the waist, her fine dress possibly ruined, she came at him with her fingernails. He grabbed her arms and held on tight. Because she was in a sort of half squat, she could not bring her feet into play. "Damn you, damn you, damn you!" she shrieked.

"Whoa there," Calhoun said. Despite his strength and her small size, she was still a handful. The bartender was right—she was a hellion.

She began to tire, though, and slowed down.
That, in turn, allowed her to start thinking again,
and she couldn't for the life of her figure out why
she was fighting so. Despite his dirty clothes and
hard eyes, Maggie figured Calhoun was not just
some saddle tramp. There was something different
about him. Something that attracted her.

Maggie quit fighting and relaxed. She smiled at
Calhoun, a real smile.

Calhoun released her, but watched her warily. She
could very well just be playing possum. She rose,
pulled off her sopping dress, and tossed it aside.
Calhoun noted that he had been right—she had no
stays; no corset either. She lifted one foot and held it
out. Calhoun unlaced and pulled off her high-top
shoe. They repeated the process on the other.

Maggie sat in the water, found the soap again,
and handed it to him. "You want the paint and all
off, you do the work," she said evenly. "But mind,
you might be powerful disappointed in the result."

He wasn't. Nor was he disappointed later, when
they made love again in the soft glow of lanterns.

Calhoun slid easily out of the bed, moving quietly
so as not to wake Maggie. He had allowed himself
four hours of sleep. Between the good meal yesterday afternoon, the bath, and the times he and Maggie
had together, he was feeling better than he had in a
long time.

He carefully opened the package and donned the
new clothes. He was a little surprised that they fit

pretty well. He was often hard to fit with store-boughts, since there was little variety in size. These were quite satisfactory, though.

He sat on the plush chair and pulled on his boots. Then he found his old clothes and took the suspenders from them and buttoned them on. Next, he emptied his pants pockets, transferring his few things to the pockets of his new trousers. When he came to the money, he counted out twenty-five dollars and set it on a small nightstand next to the bed. He got his cigarette fixings from the nightstand and stuffed them in the pocket of his striped, collarless shirt.

Last, he buckled on his gun belt. He turned for the door, but then stopped and looked back. Maggie was asleep, blankets covering only her lower half. It was a nice view, but that was not what held him there. He walked back to the table and picked up his twenty-five dollars. He stood, holding it, thinking.

Leaving the money would bring his finances down to less than five dollars. That presented a dilemma, and he had to choose. Even with the money in his hand, he had nowhere near enough cash to get himself a horse, saddle, and supplies to go hunting Bohannon and his men. There were two ways he could try to get the money: he could either go rob someplace—something he had done before when he was in dire straits, though he had never taken to it much—or try to get in a poker game. Of course, if his luck was bad, he might end up having to rob someone or someplace anyway.

What the hell, he finally thought, *I'm gonna try a poker game first.* He stuffed the twenty-five dollars in his pocket. It was not much of a start, but it was better than five dollars.

He glanced over at Maggie again. She looked great, and for a moment he regretted not leaving the money for her. Then he vowed that he would come back and repay her, whether it was later this day or after he had taken care of Bohannon's bunch.

He spun and strode out, easing the door closed behind him.

CHAPTER

✳ 16 ✳

Calhoun moved swiftly, lightly, through the house, catching snatches of whispered conversation. Downstairs, he strode past the rooms on the first floor where the women waited, but he felt certain none had seen him as he walked the length of the hallway.

He eased out the front door of Maggie's brick house. The night was muggy, though a breeze kept it from being unbearable. He turned and walked the few doors to Oldman's Saloon, hoping to find a game going on there. He was not disappointed.

Calhoun had to wait a little while before he could get into the game, seeing as how there were six men already playing. He didn't mind the wait since it afforded him a chance to observe the players. He did let it be known, though, that he wanted in on the game as soon as possible. He bought a bottle of whiskey and stood sipping from it while he watched the game.

Finally one of the men went broke and left. Calhoun was invited to sit and play. He pulled out his twenty-nine dollars and tossed the money on the table and set his bottle down. He anted and the cards came flashing toward him.

He won the first few hands for small pots, and then lost one. The next time, however, he won again, a sizable pot this time, and suddenly he had sixty-three dollars sitting in front of him. Good, but still nowhere near enough to buy all he would need to hunt down Bohannon's men.

He won a few more hands, wrapped around a couple of losses, and had almost enough as he figured he would need to do his work.

Then the cards turned cold. He was on the verge of being broke at one point, but then won two small pots to keep him in the game. His luck was suddenly short-lived again and he couldn't win anything.

He could have quit, but he pressed on for a couple of reasons. One was that he was determined at least to win back enough to pay Little Maggie. The other was that he knew for sure that one of the men was cheating. The man, who Calhoun learned was named Spence, was adept at what he was doing, but Calhoun had no doubt he was cheating.

Calhoun considered revealing his suspicions, but waited. It would not suit his purposes to have a group of enraged gamblers take Spence out and string him up from the nearest roofbeam. Soon Calhoun was down to nothing but the small change in his pockets.

"Damn, I ain't ever had a run of luck so piss poor," he announced as he stood up. He grabbed his half-empty whiskey bottle and strolled out, seemingly no more concerned than any man would be who had dropped almost thirty bucks in a card game.

Outside, he turned at the end of the building into

the pitch-black alley. There he waited, patiently, leaning against the corner of the saloon so he could see anyone coming or going from the place. He sipped only occasionally from the bottle. He judged dawn to be less than an hour off. It was still hot and clammy, and the wind that had brought a bit of coolness to the area had died down to a mere ghost of a breeze. It did little to take the edge off the heat.

Half an hour later Calhoun set the bottle down. He had had enough, and knew that even a few more sips would send him over the edge to drunkenness. He rolled a cigarette and fired it up. The streets were deserted for the most part, and the city pretty well asleep except for a couple of the saloons. Even the brothels were quiet and dark now.

Calhoun was getting impatient as a faint pink tinged the eastern sky, but soon after that, Spence strolled out of the saloon, his hat in his hand. He stopped on the wood boardwalk outside the saloon's front door and stretched, breathing in the muggy, almost still air.

Spence was a little taller than he had seemed sitting at the table, and looked wiry and fairly strong. But Calhoun also figured that he had been used to high living off his ill-gotten gambling winnings over the years, which would have softened him up some. Not that Calhoun cared. He would willingly face the devil himself if it suited his needs at the time.

Spence wore a fine black wool suit with a matching vest. Calhoun had seen inside the saloon that the gambler's shirt was white, but seemed soiled from long wear. The man wore no belt pistol, but

Calhoun figured he was heeled with a couple of small guns in his jacket or pants pockets, maybe even up his sleeve. Calhoun had seen such things before. Spence set his hat on firmly, running his fingers around the front and sides of the brim. He turned toward Calhoun, who had ducked his head just back of the corner.

Calhoun heard the footsteps coming and he braced himself. Dawn was here, though it was still fairly dark in the alley. A couple of cocks crowed from somewhere. Pawnee Flats would be coming alive soon, and he wanted to be done with his business before that.

Calhoun grabbed Spence's arm as the cardsharp stepped off the end of the boardwalk. His other hand snaked out and clamped around Spence's throat, and he hauled the cardsharp into the alley. There, he slammed him up against the saloon wall and slapped a hard hand against his chest. The other hand eased the pressure on the gambler's throat minutely.

"What the hell's going on here?" Spence asked, sounding indignant.

"I ain't got a lot of time for bullshit," Calhoun snarled. "So you best listen well."

"Um, sure," Spence allowed. He wanted to seem innocent to this madman. If Calhoun backed away at all, he figured he could get to one of his pistols. He'd make short work of Calhoun, he was certain.

"I ain't fond of card cheats at the best of times, boy. And when the goddamn cheater cleans me out, I'm even less favorably disposed toward him."

"I don't know what you're talking about, my good man," Spence said stiffly.

"You can make this easy or hard. I don't much mind which."

"What do you want?" Spence said, licking his lips. He was suddenly scared.

"A hundred bucks ought to be good."

"Why, you're nothing more than a thug. Rousting people right out in the street."

Calhoun shrugged. "Think what you want."

"Well," Spence said bravely, "I'm not about to give you that money. I don't have that much on me even if I wanted to." He hoped his lies sounded convincing. He was trying to buy time. Dawn was almost on them, and soon there would be a lot of people in the street. This man would not dare hurt him, probably not even rob him, then.

"Too bad. Then it's gonna be the hard way."

Spence almost wet his pants. There was something in Calhoun's voice that seemed to be coming straight up from the depths of hell. He had totally misread Calhoun when the new man had sat in on the card game. Oh, he could see easy enough that Calhoun was a hard man, but he didn't think him astute enough to catch his card manipulations. He figured it probably was the late hour and the long time he had played the game last night. He was very tired, and that probably affected his sizing up of Calhoun.

Still, Matt Spence had faced other angry losers before, who figured he must be cheating, even if they could not prove it. He had come through those times, and he was determined to come through this one, too. He was not about to be bullied by this thug.

"Now don't go getting itchy, friend," Spence said as Calhoun began to slide that bowie knife out.

Calhoun stopped and looked at him.

"I really don't have that much cash on me, friend," Spence said unctuously. "I left most of it with the bartender. They keep my cash for me since I spend so much time there. I don't want to be accosted by thieves, you know." He grinned weakly, showing he really meant no offense. "If you let me go, I'll go on back in the saloon and get it."

Calhoun was amazed at how stupid people could be at times. Especially ones who saw Calhoun's hard face and armament and immediately figured him for a hardcase but one with no wits.

"A hundred now," Calhoun hissed, "or I'll carve it out of you." He, too, was well aware of the time. The sounds of the awakening city were enough to warn him that speed was essential.

"Sure, sure," Spence said hastily as Calhoun finished pulling the bowie out. "You gotta let me get into my pockets, though."

Calhoun nodded and moved the hand from Spence's chest. He stepped back a pace. Spence began patting himself and reaching into pockets as if he couldn't quite remember where he had left his cash. He was still stalling for time, but knew his gambit had gone about as far as it could.

Spence moved his hand into a pocket, and he suddenly smiled. "Ah, here it is," he said with relief.

Calhoun saw the butt of the small pistol before it

was halfway out of the man's pocket. Without hesitation, he stepped up and impaled Spence's stomach on the bowie.

Spence sort of gasped and his eyes widened. He looked down and saw only the hilt of Calhoun's knife. "Shit," he whispered. Then his bladder released. Moments later an ammonialike stink emanated from his fine wool pants.

Calhoun slapped his left hand onto Spence's throat, just under the jaw, and he held the gambler up as he pulled out his knife. He swiftly wiped the blade clean on the gambler's jacket and then let him fall.

As he put his bowie away Calhoun looked out toward the street. No one was around yet, though he could hear more sounds of the city coming alive. He knew he had little time. He grabbed Spence's jacket and dragged the body toward the rear of the saloon. Just around the corner he dropped it.

Calhoun knelt alongside the dead cardsharp and began to empty his pockets. He found a marked deck of cards, two extra aces, and an assortment of small guns and knives. He placed all that atop Spence's chest, one of the guns lying on the two aces.

Calhoun continued his search and came up with almost two hundred dollars. He did not bother to count it, just stuffed the money into his pockets. Then he walked swiftly through the alley. At the corner of the saloon he turned toward Maggie's place, moving swiftly but not so much so as to attract attention.

He let himself into Maggie's, glad that the door was not locked. He walked silently down the hallway and up the carpeted stair. Easing himself into Maggie's room, he was relieved to see she was still asleep. Having thrown off her covers, she was a mighty enticing figure.

Calhoun debated a few moments what to do. He could stay dressed, wake her, and tell her he was ready to leave. Or he could strip down again, get into bed, and pretend not to have been up. That might take some doing, since he would have to make the package of new clothes look like it hadn't been opened.

Though the latter was the harder to pull off, it also had the most interesting possibilities, seeing as how Maggie's nudity was having a definite effect on him.

He pulled off his weapons and stacked them back on the floor where they had been. Then he pulled off his clothes, folding each piece and setting in the paper. He figured that if Maggie woke now, he could just say he was getting dressed.

Soon enough, he was down to the altogether. The package of clothes did not look like it had been untouched, and Calhoun figured he would just have to prevent Maggie from seeing it. He turned and eased himself into the bed. Maggie stirred with his movement, and he feigned sleep, and then pretended to wake.

"Morning," Maggie said, smiling brightly. She looked a little tired from having just woken up, but she looked good to Calhoun nonetheless.

"Mornin'."

"Coffee?" she asked.

"That'd be nice." He paused. "A little later."

"I do declare," she said, feigning surprise and batting her eyelashes at him.

After they were done, Maggie pulled the bell cord. Minutes later Mazie came in. "Yes'm?"

"Coffee for two, some eggs, and bacon."

"Yes'm." Mazie left, and Maggie snuggled up a little closer to Calhoun. She hadn't felt this good with a man in years. While she knew it could not last, she didn't want it to end soon, either.

After breakfast, coffee, and a cigarette, Calhoun stood and stretched. He headed toward the package of clothes and began getting dressed.

"You have to go already?" Maggie asked, almost petulantly.

Calhoun nodded.

"Why?"

"Business."

"What kind of business?"

Calhoun looked at her, his face stony. Maggie suddenly felt afraid. "Sorry. Didn't mean to pry."

He shrugged. When he finished dressing, he pulled some hard money from his pocket. "How much I owe you, ma'am?" he asked.

Maggie was shocked, not at the offer of money. This was, after all, her business. No, it was more the fact that he had suddenly become so distant from her. "Twenty ought to do it."

Calhoun nodded. He counted out twenty-five dollars and set it on the table. Then he leaned over, placed his palms on the bed, and kissed Maggie long and hard.

She was disconcerted. That kiss had certainly not been businesslike. "Y'all come back now, y'heah," she said breathlessly as Calhoun reached the door.

"I'll make it a point," Calhoun said.

CHAPTER

✶ 17 ✶

Calhoun strolled to the general store. He bought what supplies he would need, including a good bedroll, one with two thick blankets and waterproof canvas. While the store clerk was fetching things Calhoun grabbed a piece of hard penny candy and popped it into his mouth. He hadn't had such a thing in ages, and he felt all the better for it now since this piece had been filched. Finally he paid the clerk and told him that he would be back to get his purchases soon.

Looking like he had not a care in the world, Calhoun walked to the livery stable on the north edge of town. He figured Spence's body hadn't been found yet, since there was no activity indicating that it had.

The livery man was half-asleep, which suited Calhoun just fine. "Where's Spence's horse?" he asked.

"Huh?" the livery man said dumbly.

"I asked you where was Spence's horse."

"Who's Spence?"

"Gambler. Wears a black suit, a flat-crown hat. A real dandy."

"Ah, yeah, now I 'member. You say you want his horse?"

"Yep. Him and I're goin' up north a piece to look over some land. I just rode in last night and left my horse over by the hotel. He's gettin' us some supplies and asked if I could come down here and get his horse for him." Calhoun stopped, out of energy. He rarely spoke more than a few words at any one time. He had just given a full-fledged politicallike speech here and it was wearing on him.

"Oh, sure," the man said. "It's right back here." He led Calhoun to the third stall. "Here he is," he said, pointing to a strong-looking bay gelding. "That's his saddle, bridle, and saddlebags hangin' there on the wall."

Calhoun nodded. "Obliged. How much?"

"Buck and a half ought to do it."

Calhoun paid him and set about saddling the horse. The animal was nervous, shuffling about a little, but Calhoun managed to get him calmed down. He got the bridle on and then walked out, towing the horse behind him. Outside, he cut to the left, heading for the main street. He stopped out back of the mercantile store and got his supplies. He was traveling light, and didn't need much. Most of the things he stuffed into the saddlebags; the food he put in a burlap sack and hung it over the saddle horn.

At last he pulled himself onto the horse. Deciding the stirrups were too low for him, he adjusted them. Finally he was riding down the street, heading west. As he passed Oldman's Saloon people were rushing down the alleyway next to it. Spence's corpse had been found.

Calhoun kept riding, not showing any interest. He

did look at Maggie's place, though, and was surprised when he saw her standing in her bedroom window. She waved, and he returned it.

Calhoun wanted to be on Bohannon's trail something awful, but he knew he had to leave Pawnee Flats easily so as not to draw any attention to himself. He doubted much whether anyone in the town would be upset that a cardsharp had gotten himself knifed. But Calhoun didn't need to take a chance that he would be arrested for the murder.

Once he was out of town, he spurred the horse. Not only was he hell-bent to get on the trail of the posse, he also wanted to test the horse's capabilities. The animal looked strong and had a nice gait. Calhoun figured that a horse used by a gambler like Spence would be a good animal, for it was certain that he would frequently have to leave a town in a hurry with a posse or vigilance committee after him.

After two hours moving at a good pace, Calhoun felt the horse had proved its endurance. He eased off some then, not wanting to use the horse up so early. He was certain he would have some hard riding ahead.

Just after nightfall he reached the spot where the battle had taken place. He had come in one long day as far as he had gone in four on foot.

He grabbed some firewood by the light of the moon and soon had a fire going. He put coffee and meat on to cook as he cared for the horse. He ate quickly, neither enjoying nor hating the meal. It was simply something that had to be done, and he did it with no fuss.

He had more or less blocked out his mission on the long ride today, but as he sat puffing an after-supper cigarette it intruded on his thoughts. He could not sort out what it meant to him.

Growling angrily at himself for letting his thoughts run amok, he cleaned his pistols. He had fired the one several times before he got to Pawnee Flats and had not been able to clean it. That bothered him. He would need his pistols and would be filled with disgust if they did not operate properly because of neglect. Finally he finished, and turned in.

The next morning, after a fast breakfast, he started looking for tracks. He was glad it had not rained since the battle. There was no sign left of Medicine Bear, the scavengers having taken care of that. Nor was there much sign of the blood and such that had been shed. What surprised him was that there were no graves around. He was certain that Medicine Bear had killed at least one of the men. He shrugged. He had more important things to worry about than where Bohannon had buried his men.

It did not take long to find the group's trail. It moved westward along the Platte River. It did not surprise Calhoun—anyone who had been out here more than a few months knew the Sioux lived north of the Platte. Calhoun's job would be to find where the party of self-styled rangers crossed the wide, shallow, muddy river.

He swung in the saddle and pushed on, moving at a steady clip. There was no real need for him to check sign too closely, at least not for a while. So he stopped only about every hour. He would loosen the saddle, allowing the horse to breathe. While the horse drank or grazed, Calhoun would check the land, making sure he was still on the right trail.

Several hours later he was following the Platte when he came on a campsite the rangers had used. Here he found the graves he had not seen back at the battle site. There were three of them, covered over with stones. Each had a cross made of two willow sticks lashed together with rawhide thongs. Each also had a scrap of paper stuck under some rocks. Calhoun looked at them. Each was the same, except for the name. Calhoun learned that Lije Bates, Lonnie Cofield, and Mitch Cleland had been brutally murdered by a savage of the Sioux tribe.

Calhoun placed the papers back, and then prowled the well-used campsite. He saw sign that the children were still alive. He was a little surprised that he found no sign of Painted Sky. He was certain the rangers had taken her along. He finally decided, though, that she had been more seriously wounded than he had suspected, and had died early on along the trail. Men like Bohannon's would casually toss a dead squaw aside as if she was no more than a piece of spoiled meat. As they had with Medicine Bear's body, the scavengers would have taken care of any trace of the woman.

He also was a bit surprised to see sign that indicated that Sergeant Whitcomb and Private O'Shea were traveling with the rangers. He had been sure that they would have hightailed it to the nearest town, tossed away their uniforms, and skedaddled for parts unknown. They seemed to be the type to desert, given a decent chance of doing so safely. He could not understand it, but he did not mind. It would save him time in tracking them down if they continued on with Bohannon and the others.

He pushed on since it was still only midday. As he had before, he stopped once in a while to check the ground. The fifth time he had done that, he knelt there staring at the ground for a long time. He moved ahead a few feet and knelt again, scrutinizing the land. He stood, holding the reins loosely in his hand and staring out at the horizon. His face was hard.

Someone else was following the rangers. In and of itself, that was nothing strange. Neither was the fact that it was an Indian who was doing the following, and a Sioux. What was strange was that there was only one Sioux following the rangers.

Calhoun still stood staring, trying to puzzle it out. He supposed it could just be chance that the Indian was taking the same trail. After all, following the Platte as they all were doing was not so strange a thing to do. Still, Calhoun had a hunch that this Indian was tracking the rangers. His hunches had rarely been wrong, and he did not discount this one.

He tightened the saddle and took off, moving a little more swiftly. He wanted to catch up to whoever was out there and catch him before he got himself killed by the rangers. Not that he cared about another Sioux getting killed, but such an occurrence might force the rangers to do something to the children.

Calhoun found another campsite the men had used, and he pulled in for the night. While supper cooked he prowled, checking the sign. The children were still alive, he found. He also saw more sign that whoever was following the trail had stayed there, too, though a day or two later.

He ate, cared for the horse, and then turned in.

He pushed the horse pretty hard the next day, trying to make up ground. It had taken him almost a week between the battle and the time he was riding after the rangers. They could have covered a fair piece of ground in that time, though Calhoun had seen no signs that they were in any hurry. Still, the more time that elapsed between first seeing them and then catching up to them, the greater the chance that the two children might die. He was nearly obsessed with saving the children.

Calhoun rode to well past nightfall, fairly certain that the men had not crossed the Platte. He wondered if they might be heading for Fort Laramie, but this made no sense. If the rangers rode into the fort without Calhoun, Medicine Bear, and Painted Sky, but with the two children, there would be a heap of questions, none of them easy to answer. Of course, it could be that Bohannon was arrogant enough to figure he could bluff his way through anything.

Once again, Calhoun did the minimum chores he had to, then turned in.

Dawn was just breaking as he packed up the last of his supplies the next day. He wanted to be off and going, but he wanted enough light to see by. There was always the possibility that Bohannon's men had already crossed the Platte, which split into the north and south forks not far away. Riding out before he learned if they had done that might just cost him a lot more time than waiting a few minutes for the sunrise.

He had been right—they were still following the Platte. The day was like all the others had been since he left Pawnee Flats. It was hot, with a kind of brittleness to the constant breeze. He supposed that was better than the muggy oppressiveness of a week or so ago. Still, it was not pleasant to be riding under the hot sun, sweating like a stuck pig.

At one of his short stops to check the ground, he noticed that the horse of whoever was trailing the rangers had slowed, as if wearing out.

He began to wonder through the rest of that day, and most of the next, just what Bohannon's men were thinking. As best Calhoun could figure, it was only four or five days of hard riding to Fort Laramie.

He shook his head. He could not fathom what they were planning, and all the thinking in the world would not give him the answer.

Another hour on, he stopped and looked for sign. There was none to be found. "Damn," he muttered as he mounted his horse again. He rode back along his trail, moving slowly as his eyes searched the ground.

Finally he found the spot where they had crossed the river. He stopped and looked around, but saw little that would help him. All seemed normal, from the small herd of buffalo northeast across the river to the two hawks circling high above, looking for prey.

He eased the horse into the muddy river. Crossing the Platte always worried him. The current was constantly shifting, and there were patches of quick-sand, some of them long. Many were the folk who saw how shallow and innocent looking this river was and figured it would be easy getting across. And many were the folk who lost a horse or brace of oxen to the treacherous sandy bottom of the infernal river. Calhoun always looked at the Platte with a healthy dose of respect.

Calhoun made it safely and stopped on the north bank. The horse deserved a rest. He knelt and scooped some water into his mouth. Then he rolled and lit a cigarette as he once again surveyed the landscape.

Sand hills and short-grass prairie spread both to the north and the south. It was an unpleasant, harsh land all in all, and Calhoun was not fond of it. He preferred the wooded hollows of his native Kentucky, though he had not been back once since he had left there a decade or so ago.

Once more he hit the trail, riding slowly while watching for sign. The rangers were moving more slowly now as they edged into the real heart of Sioux country. They might talk big and even be as tough as boot leather, but they were no match for a thousand Sioux warriors, and they knew it.

Late in the afternoon Calhoun slowed. The trail signs were confusing and he needed to sort them out. He finally realized that whoever was following Bohannon and the others was barely moving. He expected to find the Indian any moment. What really befuddled him, though, was that the tracks seemed somehow familiar. He stopped and dismounted, deciding that the tracks were familiar only because he had been following them for several days.

Holding a hand over the horse's mouth, he listened intently. He heard nothing out of the ordinary, but he was certain that the Indian was around. Half a mile ahead he saw a thin curl of smoke. That meant the Indian probably was there, making an evening cookfire.

CHAPTER

* 18 *

Calhoun stopped and tied off the horse. Pulling one of the Dragoons, he edged forward. Since there was little vegetation in the series of small ravines, he bellied up closer to where he thought the Indian was, trying to make no noise. He thought he had succeeded. Finally he stopped, looking out into another small ravine. He saw the horse first, and then the Indian.

He could hardly believe his eyes as he watched Painted Sky squatting, trying to start a buffalo-chip fire. He stayed behind cover for a bit, wanting to make sure no one else was around.

The Sioux woman had the fire going and began skinning a rabbit. Calhoun could not figure out how she had gotten it with no weapons. He mentally shrugged. It was not important.

Painted Sky dangled the rabbit over the flames on a stick braced by two rocks. The she rocked back on her heels, wiping sweat off her forehead. To Calhoun, she seemed completely exhausted. Still with his Dragoon in hand, he stepped out from the brush.

"That'll go a heap better with coffee," he said quietly.

Painted Sky jumped up and turned, reaching for

the knife in her belt. Her face was a feral mask of rage.

Calhoun rose and put up a hand. "I come to help you, Painted Sky," he said.

Painted Sky stopped, looking at him as if seeing a ghost. She was frightened, but not too much. This man had not harmed her before. Indeed, he had helped her a few times. Still, he was a white eyes, like the ones who had carried off her children. As such, he could not be trusted, at least not yet.

Painted Sky nodded and left her knife in the sheath. "You have coffee?"

Calhoun nodded. "Sugar, too." That would get her, he figured. She loved sugar in her coffee, he had learned soon after leaving Fort Laramie. That seemed like a lifetime ago.

"I share." It was both a statement, offering him some of the rabbit, and a question about his coffee.

"I share, too." Calhoun slid the Dragoon away and turned. A few minutes later he was back with his horse and was pulling the small coffeepot and the coffee out. He handed them both to her, and she quickly had the coffee beans smashed and sitting in the coffeepot full of water.

Calhoun sat on a rock near the fire and rolled a cigarette. "I thought you was dead," he said. "Or took off by them villains."

Painted Sky shook her head, her long, raven-black hair swinging freely. "I shot, but only little," she said. She pulled down the top of her dress on one side, exposing a breast as she had done when breast-feeding Red Arrow. This time, though, she half turned.

Calhoun nodded when he saw the ugly line of marred flesh high up on the shoulder. "It all right now?" he asked. Judging by the look of the wound, she was just fine.

"Yes," she said firmly. She redid her dress. "I rode some and then fall off horse." She paused, trying to figure out the words to use with her far-from-perfect command of English. "I crawl into brush along river and hide from the white eyes till they go by. Then I catch horse again."

Calhoun nodded, looking her over. It was the first time he had really done so. She was plenty attractive, even in her soiled buckskin dress and with dirt and sweat all over her face.

"White eyes take Fat Bear and Red Arrow," she said, voice wobbling a little as she fought back tears.

Calhoun puffed his cigarette, looking off into the distance. He could not look at her now. Not when she was quietly sobbing for the loss of her children. He knew just how she felt, and it no longer mattered to him that she was of the hated Sioux tribe. Beyond that, she was simply a mother grieving for her children, who had been carried off by rough and dangerous men and might be dead by now.

He still hated the Sioux. Nothing would ever change that, but he decided then and there that he would not hate *all* the Sioux. He figured he could make an exception for this nice-looking young woman who had lost her youngsters. He still felt nothing but hatred for her husband, though Medicine Bear had been killed and mutilated.

"Then you followed?"

"Yes. I go slow, follow. Wait."

"Waitin' till you got back to your people?" Calhoun said more than asked. It made sense. She could do nothing about a band of seven armed men when she had only a knife. But if they got closer to her homeland, she could get her people and point out the enemy. The Sioux warriors would do the rest.

"Yes." She nodded. She began to relax a little as her certainty that this man was a friend and not an enemy grew. He was a white eyes, yes, she knew, but he was not like the others. Still, she sensed something in him that kept her a little edgy.

"They take the young'uns to trade 'em for captives?" Calhoun asked.

"Yes. I hear. They say so. If that not work, they say they use children for . . ." Her face scrunched up as she tried to find the words.

"For bait?" Calhoun asked.

Painted Sky looked at him, a question in her eyes.

Calhoun had been so surprised at her command of English that he was suddenly flummoxed when she could not understand such a simple word. He wondered where she had learned what English she did know. It was unusual for an Indian woman to know the white man's language.

"Ah, bait," he said again. Using signs and gestures, he managed to get the idea across that the men would be willing to use the children to draw some Indians, guilty or not, into a trap.

Painted Sky nodded vigorously. "Yes, yes," she responded. "They say they do that. Or kill them."

Her face curled up again as she fought against the tears. She could not hold them back, though.

"Dammit," Calhoun muttered. The sight of this woman grieving for her small children who might be dead made him look at his own hatred for Indians a little more closely. What he saw was not pleasant. He steeled himself against her sobs. It was made easier when he pictured in his mind's eye the burning farmstead and the two rent bodies. Yes, he decided, he could still hate the Sioux as deeply as ever.

A picture of a chubby little Indian sitting in his lap suddenly intruded in his grief, and he shook his head, trying to erase it, but he could not. *Yes,* he thought, *I can hate the Sioux. But I don't have to hate every Sioux.*

"We'll get your boys back, Painted Sky," he said quietly.

Painted Sky wiped away her tears, though she continued to sob. Still, she looked at him, heart hoping he spoke the truth, head telling her he was a white man like all the others. She nodded. "You help?" she asked.

Calhoun nodded, too. "It's why I come all this way," he said flatly.

"Why?" she asked.

That baffled Calhoun, and it was some time before he spoke, trying to put some reasoning into why he was here. After all, it made as little sense to him as it probably did to her.

"Those bastards took my horse and saddle," he said flatly. He hoped he sounded more convincing to her than he did to himself. "Plus one of 'em smacked me a good shot on the head." His words staggered to a halt.

Painted Sky seemed to believe him, though. It was right for a man to chase after others who had stolen his horse. It made perfect sense to the Sioux woman. "Why you hate me?" she asked.

Her changing of topics so swiftly confounded Calhoun. He looked at her in some surprise. "I don't hate you, ma'am," he said politely.

"I see in eyes you hate me."

"I don't hate you," Calhoun repeated. He paused. "I do hate your people, though."

"Why?"

Calhoun sat there and glared at her. He did hate her at this moment, for trying to pry into his life like that. "None of your damn business," he finally said.

Painted Sky nodded, sadness falling over her again.

"That rabbit about done?" Calhoun asked, trying to fill the dead air with some sound.

Painted Sky leaned forward and prodded the roasting meat with a stubby, dirty finger. "Done," she announced.

Calhoun poured coffee into his mug. "We share," he said.

Painted Sky nodded and cut off a piece of meat. Calhoun did the same. They ate silently. When they finished, he made a cigarette. Then, slowly, haltingly, in short clipped sentences, he told Painted Sky why he hated the Sioux. He had no idea of why he did it, and he felt no better about it once he was done.

Painted Sky, though, stared at him, her soft almond eyes filled with tears again. She had learned that all white men were bad; evil men who stole Sioux children and raped Sioux women. They killed Sioux warriors for no reason, and they lied whenever they spoke. So she had learned.

Now she looked at Calhoun and saw in his eyes the pain he felt, and she knew he spoke truthfully. She felt sorry for him and was sympathetic about his loss. "I sorry," she said, knowing that was inadequate, but wanting him to know she felt for him.

Calhoun nodded and flung a cigarette butt into the fire. He was disgusted with himself for having spoken. The only things he could think of that mitigated his weakness were the knowledge that he would never see Painted Sky again, once this business was done with, and the fact that his speech would not change anything. Lizbeth and Lottie would still be dead, and he would still hate most of the Sioux and they him. There would be no fewer Sioux raids on whites, no fewer attacks on Sioux by white men.

He pushed up. Without saying anything, he got his bedroll and flapped it open. Using his saddlebags as a blanket, he lay down and closed his eyes. It took some time to get to sleep, but he finally managed to slay the demons that were keeping him awake.

In the morning Calhoun had coffee going before Painted Sky even woke. She felt guilty when she finally rose. She was a poor excuse for a woman, she thought as she set about making breakfast.

Calhoun did not blame her. She had traveled a long way, with a wound, and full of worry for her children. For the first time in almost two weeks she had been able to sleep in relative safety.

As he sat to breakfast Calhoun said, "I looked over your horse. He's near played out."

"Played out?" Painted Sky asked, stymied by the strange expression.

"It's near about dead on its feet," Calhoun said flatly.

"Oh." Painted Sky kind of stared out into nowhere as she thought about that. Then she nodded firmly. "I walk," she said.

Calhoun shook his head. "Nope. We'll ride double."

"Yes?"

"Yep. He's a good strong horse and should be able to carry us both. Besides, I don't reckon we'll be goin' too far?"

"They close," Painted Sky said firmly.

They damn well better be, Calhoun thought. He said nothing, though.

Finished eating, Painted Sky began cleaning up while Calhoun saddled the big bay. Finally they were ready. Calhoun mounted, and then pulled his left foot out of the stirrup and held out his left hand.

Painted Sky grabbed his hand and stepped into the stirrup. With a yank, Calhoun pulled her up onto the horse behind him. "You all right back there?" he asked.

"Yes."

He nodded and rode out of the camp. He picked

up the trail right away. He thought he and Painted Sky would run down Bohannon's men this day, but it was not to be. He pulled to a stop in the late afternoon, in a shallow depression in the rolling prairie land. They had moved away from the creek early in the day, and there was nothing out here but the emptiness, as far as they could see.

While Calhoun unsaddled and groomed the horse Painted Sky went about picking up buffalo chips for a fire. Calhoun dug a small hole in the mostly northern side of the coulee. Painted Sky built a small fire in the hole. It protected the meager flames both from the considerable wind that had sprung up as well as from the eyes of anyone who might be around.

Along with the wind had come a thick overcast. Just as they were finishing supper the rain started.

"Shit," Calhoun commented. He was annoyed, as seemed to be the case almost constantly these days. He got his bedroll and laid it out. "Get in," he said.

Painted Sky looked at him blankly. "You?" she asked.

"I'll sleep settin' up." He wished he had his own saddlebags. With his slicker, he would be almost comfortable.

"No," Painted Sky said.

"Ain't no use in both of us gettin' soaked," Calhoun said in exasperation.

"We share," Painted Sky said firmly.

Calhoun looked at her sharply, wondering. Then he shrugged. For a moment there he had thought she wanted to share more than just a bedroll, but he knew now he must be mistaken.

They climbed into the covers, pulling the blankets and canvas up over their heads. A few minutes later Calhoun heard Painted Sky's soft snoring. It took him a little while to relax, but then he, too, fell asleep.

CHAPTER

✳ 19 ✳

Calhoun was glad the rain had stopped overnight. It would have wiped out a lot of tracks already, and picking them up again could take some doing. He just hoped there were some tracks left for him to find.

However, since the clouds had broken off and drifted away, the sun was able to beat down with full force. Calhoun felt he was damned either way. If it rained, he lost the tracks; if it was sunny, he sweltered and choked on dust. It seemed to be a way of life with him.

When he and Painted Sky left, Calhoun kept the horse at a walk, not wanting to hurt the animal, what with both him and Painted Sky riding on it. The slow pace also allowed Calhoun to keep a close eye on the trail of the men he was following. Because of that, he caught the trail of some of the men turning west. Calhoun swung that way and followed it a little. Then he stopped.

"Wrong?" Painted Sky asked from behind him.

"A couple of 'em've gone this way."

"Who?"

"The soldier boys." Calhoun wanted to find Whitcomb and O'Shea here and now, and so he sat there fighting the itch to do so. He finally managed to conquer it. He pulled the bay horse around and headed back to the main trail.

He was irritated all the time now. He had been on the trail too long, following these demons without success. He wanted to get it over with, pay the bastards back as soon as possible for the trouble they had caused him. So he was not real happy when Painted Sky slumped against him. It was annoying for him to have to sit straight up with her deadweight against him. Then he realized she was asleep. He bit back his annoyance. She had come through a heap of hard times lately, and he was not going to increase her burden, even if she was a Sioux.

As Calhoun rode he wondered if he had made the right decision in going after Bohannon and his men rather than the two soldiers. He hated those two more than he did Bohannon and his men. Or did he? He was not sure he could answer that question honestly. Whitcomb and O'Shea both had tried to kill him more than once, and they were the ones who had clubbed him in the back of the head and left him to die. That was a heap of troubles to pay back for.

On the other hand, Bohannon's men hadn't exactly done too much to Calhoun directly. However, any group of men who took to stealing children for their own ends were pretty low-down folks to Calhoun's thinking. And if that wasn't enough, they would have killed him, and Painted Sky, too, he was sure, had the situation been a little bit different.

Trying not to move too much and disturb Painted Sky, Calhoun rolled a smoke. As he puffed away he tried to force his mind away from useless thoughts. It was simple. He had to rescue the children first. Then and only then could he set about killing the men who had done him—and Painted Sky—so much harm.

Painted Sky roused after an hour or so and yawned. "You feelin' better now?" Calhoun asked.

"Yes. Good." She still sounded worried, though, and Calhoun wished there were something more he could do to help her. He stopped soon after to give the horse a short rest. The two of them made do with a bit of jerky and some hard biscuits. Since water was often hard to come by out here, they drank sparingly from the two canteens Calhoun had brought with him.

Then it was back in the saddle and more plodding miles across a land that looked as untouched now as the day the Lord had created it. There were few signs of life—all of it animal life of one sort or another. Several massive herds of buffalo moved lazily as they grazed, unconcerned about these two puny things on an old horse.

"Buffalo good," Painted Sky said, tapping Calhoun on the shoulder and pointing to a smaller herd that lagged behind the vastly larger one.

Calhoun nodded. "Buffalo good. But we can't get none now. Only way I got to kill one is with my pistol. That means gettin' right up close to one. It also means those bastards out there might hear."

"No buffalo now," Painted Sky said firmly.

Calhoun wondered what the woman was thinking. He wondered if she knew the grave danger her sons were in. These were vicious, heartless men when it came to Indians. He figured Fat Bear, the elder, would be all right, unless he had too much of his father in him. He had seemed a smart boy, though, and Calhoun figured the youngster was alive, and hopefully not hurt too much.

Calhoun's real concern was for Red Arrow, the little one. Unlike white mothers, Indian women did not wean their children young. Red Arrow was still being suckled, even at two years old. Since he had been without his mother's milk for two weeks or so now, he might've become really burdensome to Bohannon's men. They would not be the kind of men to look favorably on a squalling Indian brat, not when they had another one they could use, and that one not as troublesome.

None of it looked good for the two boys, and Calhoun hoped they were being good. The better they behaved, the easier it would be on them, relatively speaking.

Urgency began pushing Calhoun a little harder, and in turn he pushed the horse harder. He sensed that if they did not find the boys soon, it would be too late.

They did not find their prey that day either, and as they made a poor camp in another shallow depression in the plains, Calhoun wondered if somehow he hadn't gotten off the track. Finding the soldiers' trail leading west was fortuitous, considering the rain the night before. If it hadn't been for one odd hoofprint that had not been washed out, he might not have found it.

Still, he thought he had seen traces of the other group's passage, but now he was suddenly unsure of that. As Painted Sky made a small fire of buffalo chips and cooked salted beef and a pot of coffee, Calhoun stood on the flats above the small depression, looking every which way, trying to spot something, anything that would make him believe he was on the right track.

Calhoun had trouble getting to sleep again that night, which was unusual for him. He mostly went to sleep as soon as his head hit whatever it was he was using for a pillow. Now that he thought about it, this whole journey had been unusual—him traveling with a hated Sioux warrior; him learning to like two young Sioux boys; him helping Painted Sky; being knocked out by a dumb soldier, and a private to boot; losing tracks. "Damn, boy," he told himself silently, "you ought to just shoot yourself and get it over with." Only his pride kept him going. He had vowed to help Painted Sky find her children and then punish the bastards who had done all this.

Morning came, as it always did, but Calhoun did not feel very refreshed. He slurped down coffee and ate his meager breakfast without much enjoyment. He quickly saddled the horse and set the bridle over the animal's head. He was surprised that the horse had not given out by now. Considering his luck with horses, the extra weight the animal was carrying, and the long days, it was somewhat amazing.

He pulled Painted Sky up onto the horse, and

they rode off. He rode in a lazy zigzag, eyes looking for sign. He felt considerably relieved when he found it, though he did not indicate his relief. He urged the horse into moving a little faster, almost as if he were being pulled in that direction. The sensation gladdened him. It seemed that whenever he faced a task like this and that odd feeling, the itchy sense of urgency, came over him, he knew he was near.

He didn't know what made him stop sometime midway through the afternoon. Maybe it was the way some birds flew, chattering angrily, from a stand of trees down in a gully half a mile or more away. Maybe it was the heartbeat's length of time he thought he had seen a curl of smoke down there. Maybe it was the fact that the copse was the first shelter of any kind he had seen for more than two days. Or maybe it was his instincts.

Whatever it was, he stopped. "Get down," he ordered Painted Sky. Without question, she did as she was told. Calhoun stood in the stirrups shading his eyes with a hand, since his battered old hat was not quite up to the job. He sensed that his quest was near to completion. Or at least the first part of it.

He stayed there for some moments, scouting out the land, taking in things he was not even certain he saw, but they registered. "Come on, woman," he said, holding out his hand.

Painted Sky looked up at him a moment and thought she noticed something different in his posture, or his face, or voice. Maybe all of them. She knew something had caught his attention. She knew enough not to question him. She simply grabbed his hand and let him help her up onto the horse.

Painted Sky was a little surprised when Calhoun did not race off, since he seemed to be tense enough to want to do that. Then she realized that if they did that, the dust the horse kicked up would give them away to anyone who was out there. Walking the horse raised little dust, and that was quickly dispersed by the wind.

Calhoun was certain that his prey was down there in that copse. He worried that they might be seen, but that seemed unlikely—unless someone was down there watching with a telescope. And if they were, there was nothing he could do to prevent it now anyway.

An hour later they came on a small, crooked stream. Calhoun wasn't sure what it was. Painted Sky probably had a name for it, but he'd never be able to understand it anyway. He stopped and let the horse drink from the slow-moving water. He pulled the canteen from the saddle horn and handed them behind him to Painted Sky. "Best fill these while we got the chance," he said. "We might need 'em."

Painted Sky did not see any reason to answer, so she just did as she was told. Calhoun stayed up on the horse, looking around, figuring out the lay of the land. Behind him there was nothing but miles of empty, rolling terrain cut through with ravines and sand hills. Ahead was the river, and then a forest. How extensive it was, Calhoun did not know, but he figured it was fairly long along the watercourse, but was probably not very wide. The prairie was jealous of its nakedness and did not favor those who dared to try to cover her.

Painted Sky returned with the canteens and handed them to Calhoun, who hung them over the saddle horn. He helped Painted Sky up and they splashed across the wide, shallow river.

They entered the trees, each grateful for the shade, which cut the temperature by several degrees, at least. Even better, they were out of the glare of the harsh sun. That, too, was a relief.

Calhoun kept the horse at a slow walk. No matter how much he wanted to kill Bohannon and his crew, he did not want to just wander into their camp absently. He stopped every several minutes and listened hard, and sniffed the air.

It was the horse, though, who told him that they were near a camp. The animal's ears pricked up, and he shook his shaggy mane, champing at the bit. Calhoun pulled to a halt and patted the horse's neck a moment, whispering, "Good boy."

Calhoun helped Painted Sky down, and then dismounted. He stood with his hand over the horse's nose and cocked his head, listening. Then he nodded.

"They there?" Painted Sky asked in a whisper.

Calhoun nodded. "Somebody's there," he answered in kind. "Can't be sure it's them, though."

He looked around, but found no likely place to penetrate the forest farther. They were on something of a path, but Calhoun figured it went straight to the camp of whoever was out there. With a shrug, he turned and forced his way past leafy bushes, trying to disturb the foliage as little as possible. He kept a tight grip on the reins as the horse walked behind him.

Painted Sky saw what he was doing, and how careful he was being. She thought that good. As she followed the horse she did a little to try to keep the noise of the two humans and the horse a little less.

Calhoun finally found a small clearing, just about big enough for the horse and three or four people. Thick trees grew fairly tall, blotting out much of the sun's bright rays. A few humped-up boulders, dumped there in some bygone age, formed a wall on one side.

Calhoun tied the horse to a tree, filled a nose bag with the last of his grain, and hung it on the animal's head. He did it as much to keep the beast quiet as he did to reward it. Then he loosened the saddle. He did not want to take the saddle off in case they needed to get out of there in a hurry. As it was now, he could tighten up the cinch in a moment and they could be on their way.

Finally he turned to Painted Sky. "Stay here," he said. "Don't make no noise, and no fire. Understand?"

She wasn't sure she understood all the words, but she nodded anyway. She was a good Sioux woman, who knew that she should not bring attention to them or their hideout. She suspected that that was what Calhoun was saying, even if the words were unfamiliar to her.

Calhoun sat on a fallen log and pulled off his

spurs. He tossed them to Painted Sky. He was surprised when she caught them easily. As she put the spurs into his saddlebags he checked both Colt Dragoons. He made sure the two extra cylinders in his pouch were ready. He considered checking his backup gun, but then decided it was better to keep it a secret.

Calhoun nodded at Painted Sky. She smiled in return. Then he disappeared into the brush. A few yards on, he stopped and checked the cut-down Walker at the small of his back. It was sometimes a problem back there, when he was sweating a lot. This sometimes soaked through the holster and dampened the power. It was fine now, though. He put it back and pulled his shirt down over it.

CHAPTER

* 20 *

Calhoun moved through the trees and undergrowth with practiced ease and quiet, going
swiftly though not recklessly. Still, it was slow
going. He stopped every several feet and listened.
Within five minutes of leaving Painted Sky, he could
hear horses and a low buzz of men talking. He was
not close enough to understand what they were saying, or even what language they were speaking. It
was enough to know that they were out there. He
would find out who they were soon enough.

The voices grew a little louder with each yard he
put behind him. It quickly became apparent that
they were speaking English. It had to be Bohannon
and his men. No other white men would be fool
enough to be out here in the heart of Sioux country.

Calhoun had to admit that they were a tough
bunch. It took a lot of gumption to come out here in
such small numbers. They must have had some
practice in it, he figured, since they were making far
less noise than most other groups would have. They
reminded him of Texas Rangers, and he supposed a
few of them might have ridden with that tough outfit
for a spell.

Not that that meant a damn thing to Calhoun. To

him, they were dead men, plain and simple. Not only had they stolen the Sioux children to use as bait, but they were invading Sioux land. If they were not stopped, they were going to stir up a hornet's nest of trouble. If the damn fools roused the Sioux with trickery, the Sioux would pay back in kind, but ten times worse. The self-styled ranging company was jeopardizing the whole frontier. Instead of heading off more troubles like the ones that had brought them here, they were inviting more.

Calhoun slowed until he was barely inching along. The voices were clear enough for him to pick out different speakers. He could hear words, too, though none of them was saying anything important enough for him to think about.

Suddenly he stopped, as if frozen. His eyes were glued to a six-foot-long, fat rattler who was coiled up and buzzing like a hive of bees. Sweat trickled down from under Calhoun's hat as he eased out the bowie knife. He'd rather shoot the snake, but that would alert Bohannon's men, and any element of surprise would be lost. Most likely that would make him as dead as the snake's bite would.

To his great relief, the snake decided it had scared this tall skinny creature enough. It uncoiled and slithered into the brush. Calhoun remained there for some minutes, making sure the snake had plenty of time to get away. He had no desire to face it again. Snakes did not bother him, and under normal circumstances, he would have been happy to blast the thing to kingdom come. Right now, though, he just wanted to blast several two-legged serpents.

He moved on again, slowly, until the voices were quite clear. He smelled smoke and horses and roasting meat. He hadn't had a good meal in a couple of days, and the aroma of the meat made his stomach growl in hunger.

Calhoun went to his right a little, angling for a short, thick cottonwood surrounded by several leafy bushes. He stopped and looked out at a small pleasant glade. It was an ideal campsite, well protected by trees and shrubs, close enough to the water, yet out of sight. There was plenty of water and forage for the horses, and abundant firewood. He figured that a good amount of game could be had nearby, too.

Calhoun saw Bohannon first. The hard-jawed man was sitting on the ground near the fire. He had a cigarette in one hand and a tin mug of coffee in the other. And he was leaning back casually against Calhoun's saddle. *Another debt to be paid,* Calhoun thought.

Calhoun slowly surveyed the camp. The two boys were alive, he saw, though both were tied to a tree. They looked thoroughly tired and scared. He couldn't tell if they had been abused any. None of that mattered much. The important thing now was that they were alive.

Carefully Calhoun found all seven men, none of whom he knew by name except for Bohannon. They were spread out fairly well, but taking no extraordinary precautions. One was near the horses, hard to Calhoun's right. Another was keeping watch at the edge of the glade diagonally from the horses. Two men were seated at the same fire as Bohannon. The last two were nearest Calhoun, sitting at another fire, their backs to him.

Hatred smoldered in Calhoun's cold eyes, and rage flowed in his veins. He eased out both Colt Dragoons. He slid back the hammers smoothly. Each made a soft snicking sound, but it was muffled by the other normal sounds of life here.

Calhoun took in one long breath and let it dribble out. Then he stepped around the tree and strode into the camp. He fired the Dragoons alternately, snapping shots off.

The two sitting with their backs to him went down first, spines shattered before they even knew there was someone around. The powerful .44-caliber slugs knocked them forward, one into the fire, the other a foot to the side of the flames.

Bohannon was next, since Calhoun figured him the most dangerous of the bunch. He put two slugs into the man's chest.

Calhoun spun to his right and took care of the horse guard, the lead ball tearing out the man's throat. A fount of blood spurted out as he fell.

Calhoun was not paying attention. He had swung back, checking the two men who had been sitting with Bohannon. They had been sitting sideways to Calhoun and were just beginning to move, unsure of what was happening, dazed by the sudden eruption of gunfire.

Calhoun continued spinning to his left and blasted the other guard a heartbeat after the man had fired his rifle in the intruder's direction. The guard whirled, his rifle flying away. He hit a tree, bounced off, and fell to the ground, his hands jerking spasmodically.

The two nearest Bohannon were up. One headed for the brush, and Calhoun shot him low in the back, breaking a couple ribs and tearing out a chunk of his kidney. The man fell forward and tried to crawl away, but he was finding it next to impossible.

The last swung toward Calhoun, his face white with fear. He tossed his pistol down. "Don't shoot me, mister. Don't shoot!" he shouted.

"Why not?" Calhoun asked harshly, blood lust still powering him.

"I didn't want nothin' to do with this shit. I didn't!"

"Should've thought of that before you hooked up with this goddamn rabble," Calhoun snarled. He shot the man in the left knee.

"Oh, sweet Jesus," the man muttered as the shattered leg gave out on him.

As Calhoun walked toward the man he changed the spent cylinders in his Colts for fresh ones. It had been less than half a minute since he had stepped into the camp. Calhoun stopped next to the man. "I'm a man of limited patience at the best of times," he said. He slid one pistol away, then shrugged and did the same with the other. No one here was going to hurt him.

"What do you want from me?" the man asked. He was shaking from fear and pain.

Calhoun rolled a cigarette and fired it up. "I'm gonna ask you a question or two. I expect answers without a load of bullshit."

"But what if I don't know the answers?" The man's eyes were big, and his voice quavered.

Calhoun shrugged. "What's your name, boy?"

"Bo Gardner."

"You fellers abuse them two Injin boys any?"

"I didn't. I swear. Cal did some and Lee Jackson."

"Why'd Bohannon take 'em?"

"To trade for white captives. If that didn't work—Jesus, my leg hurts, mister. Can't you give me somethin'?"

Calhoun shook his head. "The kids?"

"Ah, yeah. If we couldn't trade 'em for captives, Cal figured to use 'em to set a trap for the Sioux."

"Where's the two soldier boys?"

"Went back to Fort Laramie. Or so they said."

"Why?"

"Said they wanted to desert, but they didn't have no money." He sucked in a breath as pain flared in his shattered kneecap again. "The sergeant there, he said he had some cash hid out somewhere around the fort. The other'n said he wanted the steady pay awhile longer. Then he'd skedaddle."

"Anything else you want to get off your chest?" Calhoun asked flatly.

Gardner looked up into the cold, hard eyes and a shiver ran down his spine. He opened his mouth to plead for mercy, but those eyes stopped him. There was no mercy in those two dark orbs. He knew he was going to die, and any pleading he did would serve no other purpose but to lower him even more in his executioner's eyes. He had never been a craven coward, though in the past few years he had come close to it on occasion. He was determined now to die bravely and with dignity, not groveling. He shook his head.

Calhoun shot the man in the forehead. He holstered the Dragoon and turned to the boys. "You all right, Fat Bear?" he asked as he began untying the youngster.

The boy nodded solemnly and pointed proudly to his arm. Some blood trickled down from a bullet burn on his biceps.

"That the only hurt you got?"

Fat Bear nodded. He didn't think he needed to talk about the cuffings he had received from the white men, or the scratches from brush, or the strange noises his stomach made from hunger.

"How about little Red Arrow?"

"Not hurt."

Calhoun nodded. He pointed. "Your ma's back in the brush there, by the big rocks."

Fat Bear needed no encouragement. He raced away, crashing through the foliage, shouting happily in Sioux. Calhoun assumed the boy was calling his mother's name.

"You stay here, boy," Calhoun said quietly, patting little Red Arrow on the head. Then he stood and began dragging the bodies out in the copse and dropping them off. Before he was finished, Painted Sky and Fat Bear were back, and the horse Calhoun had stolen in Pawnee Flats was with the other animals. Painted Sky was sitting, breast-feeding Red Arrow. Calhoun shook his head. It seemed to him that this would've been a good time to wean the boy, but it was not his problem, so he said nothing.

Calhoun knelt to check his saddle. It had some of Bohannon's blood on it, but otherwise was little damaged. It showed some signs of neglect, and Calhoun set about correcting that. By the time he finished, Painted Sky was making a meal from the almost fresh buffalo meat she had found among the rangers' supplies.

Calhoun sat and began cleaning his pistols. Red Arrow waddled over and stood there, standing and watching him much as his brother had done one time. Calhoun looked at the child and winked. The toddler giggled, then pointed his finger at Calhoun and made a shooting sound over and over.

Calhoun tried to smile at Red Arrow, but he could not.

Painted Sky called softly for her younger son, and he tottered away toward her. Soon after, Calhoun was done with his guns, and they were all eating.

It was a restless night for Calhoun, not because of the killing that had taken place, but because of the two boys. They had been put through some hellacious times, and it would mark them permanently. He didn't want any youngster to face that.

Finally he sighed. He could do nothing more for the children, except possibly help them get back to their people. They had their own lives to live; and so did he. He fell asleep.

The morning meal was a little easier for everyone, now that they had sort of readjusted to each other again. Calhoun ate with a renewed appetite, and then rolled a cigarette. As he sipped coffee he asked

Painted Sky, "What'm I gonna do with you three?"

"I go back to my people," Painted Sky said.

Calhoun nodded. "Take what food and other such goods as you'll need. Take all the horses, too, except the one we came here on and the one I got at Fort Laramie."

"Fort Laramie, yes," she said excitedly.

That surprised Calhoun. "You want to go to Fort Laramie?" he asked, figuring she wasn't sure of what she was trying to say.

"Fort Laramie yes." She nodded definitively.

"Your people camped there?"

"Fort Laramie, yes."

Calhoun nodded. If that's where she wanted to go, that's where he would take her, since he was planning to get there just as soon as he could. He wanted to get Whitcomb and O'Shea before they fled.

He tossed the dregs of his coffee into the fire. "Then we best get a move on," he said, rising. He looked at Fat Bear. "Come help me, boy," he said gruffly.

An hour later they were riding out of the campsite, through the clumps of trees and back onto the prairie. Calhoun felt somewhat better now that he had an extra horse and his own saddle back. That, plus getting back the weapons on the saddle, made him as happy as he ever got, though one could not tell it by looking at him.

Painted Sky had a horse now, the one Bohannon had used, as did Fat Bear. Red Arrow was a bit too small yet to ride on his own, but Calhoun figured it wouldn't be much longer before the boy would be riding like a warrior. The thought saddened him a little.

The rest of the horses were strung out behind Painted Sky and Fat Bear. Several were packed with supplies. Calhoun figured the little family would be pretty rich once they got back among their people.

CHAPTER

* 21 *

Calhoun rode into Fort Laramie and stopped in front of Major Miles Mangum's office. During the long, dusty trek back to the post, he had decided to forget his silent vow to kill the man. Calhoun had no friends, and so he figured that he could not afford to lose any of the very few men who were more than passing acquaintances to him. Besides, once he thought about it, Mangum had been more than fair with him. Most other post commanders would have let him hang.

He dismounted, stopping long enough to look over the compound. He saw no sign of either Whitcomb or O'Shea.

Half an hour ago Calhoun had sat on the rise above the Sioux camps and watched as Painted Sky, Fat Bear, and Red Arrow rode down to meet their people. He could not be convinced to make that little journey with them. He wanted no more part of the Sioux now than he had before. Just because he had become friendly with three members of the tribe did not mean he had given up hating them. It was, he admitted to himself, a little harder hating the Sioux now, but all he had to do was conjure up the picture of his old farmstead to bring the hatred back to a boil.

Then he had ridden down to the fort. He patted the horse a minute. It was the one he had taken in Pawnee Flats. His other horse—the spavined old nag Noble had saddled him with—was now a Sioux war pony. Or perhaps a Sioux feast. He didn't much care. He had enough trouble with one horse; if he had two, he figured he'd have twice the problems.

He turned and walked up the stairs. As always when Mangum was in his office, a guard stood outside, rifle in hand. The young man was staring at Calhoun as if he were the devil. "Somethin' wrong with you, boy," Calhoun asked, annoyed.

He shrugged when he got no answer. He pushed open the door to Mangum's office and strode in. The major looked up and his jaw dropped. "Calhoun!" he exclaimed. "What the . . .? How'd you . . . ? Where'd you . . . ?"

"What the hell's wrong with you, Major?" Calhoun asked, his irritation increasing rapidly.

"You're dead," Mangum was finally able to say.

"Not hardly." Calhoun walked around the desk, pulled open Mangum's bottom drawer, and got the bottle of whiskey. He worked the cork out and tossed it on the desk. Then he tilted the bottle and poured some of the fine Kentucky sour mash down into him.

Calhoun whistled. "Damn, that's good," he said flatly. Although he wasn't feeling anywhere near as cheerful as he seemed, he figured that to come stomping in here and demanding the heads of Whitcomb and O'Shea would get him nowhere, especially since Mangum must have known he was furious at him for forcing him to take on the odious task of escorting Medicine Bear to Fort Kearny. He held the bottle out. "Looks like you need this more'n me," he said calmly.

Mangum took the bottle and made a fair portion of it disappear. Then he set the bottle down on the desk.

Calhoun opened a box on the desk and pulled out two cigars. He tossed one to the major. He bit off the end of his own and lit it. Puffing like a steam engine heading up a steep grade, he sat. He stretched out his legs, crossed at the ankles. "Now, what's this shit about me bein' dead?" He had an inkling.

"Sergeant Whitcomb and Private O'Shea got back here almost a week ago. They said you all were jumped by Pawnees only a day's ride or so from Fort Kearny. They said you were killed. Medicine Bear, too. They didn't know about the woman and kids, but they thought the three of them were taken captive." Mangum paused to stare at the smoldering end of his cigar. He took another drink of whiskey.

"They said they hauled ass out of there, running for their lives. According to them, they were lucky to get away, seeing as how the whole of the Pawnee Nation was after them, and made their way back here as quickly as they could."

"You bought that pile of buffalo shit?"

"I discounted a good portion of it as exaggeration. Hell, any man's come through some kind of battle likes to tell it as if he was the goddamn hero, and if it wasn't for them, the world would've come to an end."

Mangum paused again, taking stock of his thoughts. "I was sure you'd gone over the divide, though, Wade. That much of their story had the ring of truth about it."

"I suppose it did."

"So what really happened?"

Calhoun told him, without embellishments. The major listened throughout, saying nothing, though his face revealed his swiftly changing emotions. When Calhoun was done, he asked, "So the woman and kids are safe?"

Calhoun nodded. "They're in that goddamn Sioux camp out there."

"All this didn't change your opinion of those Indians, then, I take it?"

"Only about three of 'em." Calhoun took a drink from the bottle and belched. "I couldn't see no women and kids manhandled like that."

"Goddamn hero," Mangum said facetiously. He smiled when Calhoun scowled at him.

The two men sat silent for a while. Then Mangum sighed, "I'll have them court-martialed in the morning. The hanging'll be the day after. I can't see any reason to delay."

"No," Calhoun said flatly.

"No?" Mangum snapped, certain he knew where this was going. "What the hell do you mean no?"

"I think you understand a simple word like 'no,' Major."

"Dammit, Wade, I can't let you go after two of my troops. Christ, word of that gets out and the army'll have my ass hoisted from the nearest goddamn flagpole. It's out of the question." He held up a hand, to fend off further assaults on his reasoning.

"It wasn't you clubbed down by those bastards. Nor you who had to track a passel of sons of bitches from here to hell and back again."

"I know what you've gone through, Wade. I—"

"You don't know jackshit about it," Calhoun said levelly.

Mangum knew that look in Calhoun's eyes, and despite the even tones Calhoun had used, the officer knew there was a warning there. He sat some minutes, fingers steepled before his face, elbows resting on the desktop.

"If it helps, why don't you check into the hospital."

"Huh?" Mangum asked, mind preoccupied. Then he realized what Calhoun was saying. "I suppose that might be possible." He paused. "Give me a day or two to work things out."

"We ain't got time. They get wind that I'm here, they're gonna hit the trail."

Mangum nodded. "Precisely."

Calhoun stopped with his cigar halfway to his mouth. It would solve a lot of problems, he figured. It would take Mangum off the hook while still leaving Calhoun free to track down the two soldiers. He had waited this long, another day or so wasn't going to make much difference. Indeed, it might even be better, since it would give Whitcomb and O'Shea a couple of days of knowing that he was hunting them.

"Deal, Major."

Mangum nodded and hoisted the bottle. They each drank, sealing the pact. Then the major asked, "Where're you planning to stay?"

Calhoun's eyes brightened a little. "Well, if old

Lester ain't got objections, I might room at his place again."

Mangum laughed. "Sly old devil."

Calhoun shoved up to his feet. "Best be on my way, then."

Mangum rose, too. "Let me walk you to the door." He stepped outside right behind Calhoun and stood in the open doorway, looking out over his parade ground.

Private Ian O'Shea was drilling with his company. During an eyes-right maneuver, he spotted a familiar-looking horse. A moment later the ghost of Wade Calhoun walked out of Major Miles Mangum's office. O'Shea broke ranks, pulling his rifle down off his shoulder. He dropped to one knee and brought the rifle up in a smooth move. He might not have killed Calhoun before, but he sure as hell would this time.

Calhoun stopped and turned back to speak to Mangum. But the major suddenly shouted, "Watch it!" Then he winced, and a moment later there was the crack of a rifle.

Calhoun whirled and spotted O'Shea. "Son of a bitch," he muttered. Yanking out a Colt, he jumped down the three stairs and raced toward the trooper.

O'Shea was trying to reload his rifle, and having the devil's own time of it. He glanced up and saw Calhoun charging toward him like a wounded buffalo. He flung the rifle aside, turned, and ran. He shoved his way through his fellow troopers, who were still trying to figure out what was going on.

Calhoun scattered soldiers as he made his way through the disoriented ranks. He finally was free of them at the far end of the parade ground from Mangum's office.

O'Shea was running full out, heading toward the Laramie River. Calhoun slammed to a stop and raised the Dragoon. He braced his right arm with his left hand and fired three times.

At least two of the balls hit O'Shea in the back. The bullets' impact knocked him forward and then down. He landed hard on his face and skidded a few feet across the dirt before stopping.

Calhoun turned, planning to head back across the parade ground. He wanted to see how Mangum was. Then he spotted Sergeant Gerard Whitcomb. The sergeant was racing on foot diagonally across the parade ground from the commissary a ways off to Calhoun's right. A lieutenant was about to mount his horse just outside Lester Wallace's store. Whitcomb knocked the officer down and leaped into the saddle. He jerked the animal's head hard around and then whipped it with the ends of the reins.

The horse bolted, kicking the officer on the ground at least once. Whitcomb bent low over the horse's neck and lashed the animal for all he was worth.

"Shit," Calhoun snapped. He jammed his pistol away and raced across the parade ground. He leaped onto his horse and jerked it around every bit as viciously as Whitcomb had. He also took note of the fact that Mangum was mounting a horse a few feet away, which meant that the officer could not have been hit very badly.

The two men charged toward the entrance of the

fort. Off in the distance Calhoun saw Painted Sky pointing at Whitcomb and screeching.

A quarter of a mile on, Calhoun and Mangum pulled up hard and watched as Painted Sky led a group of Sioux women in throwing anything handy at Whitcomb's horse.

The animal reared, nostrils flared in fright. When it came down, it was off balance. It kind of sat on its haunches and fell to the side. A horde of Sioux—most of them women—swarmed over the fallen man and horse. A moment later the horse was up and fleeing wildly.

Whitcomb, however, did not rise. It was not a pleasant thing to see, but both Calhoun and Mangum sat and watched as the Sioux hacked and chopped at him. His curses became screams of pain, and then they faded away.

Calhoun, who still had his cigar, pulled it out of his mouth. "Reckon he got better'n he deserved." Unconcerned, he turned his horse and headed back toward the fort.

Mangum watched him for a moment, and then followed him into the fort.

CLINT HAWKINS is the pseudonym of a newspaper editor and writer who lives in Phoenix, Arizona.